"Can you see who's driving?"

Noah shook his head. "Whoever it is, they're wearing a hoodie and glasses. I'm guessing it's a male by the size of the driver." He pulled out his phone and called for backup, then quickly swerved into another lane.

Sophia clutched the armrest. "This can't be the same person who kidnapped Kylie."

"No, this is different. This guy is driving aggressively. Somebody wants us to stop investigating, and apparently, he's willing to go to any lengths to make sure we stop."

Sophia cried out as the blue automobile hit them hard from behind. Noah struggled with the wheel but kept control, neatly avoiding the cars that were parked along the road. But the determined driver didn't stop the pursuit. Instead, he punched the engine and rammed them once again.

Sirens sounded in the background, but all Sophia could think of was the driver of the blue car, who was now striking them a third time, trying to force their car off the road.

Was she going to die today, right here and now, without ever seeing her sister Kylie again?

Kathleen Tailer is a senior attorney II who works for the Supreme Court of Florida in the office of the state courts administrator. She graduated from Florida State University College of Law after earning her BA from the University of New Mexico. She and her husband have eight children, five of whom they adopted from the state of Florida. She enjoys photography and playing drums on the worship team at Calvary Chapel in Thomasville, Georgia.

Books by Kathleen Tailer

Love Inspired Suspense

Under the Marshal's Protection
The Reluctant Witness
Perilous Refuge
Quest for Justice
Undercover Jeopardy
Perilous Pursuit
Deadly Cover-Up
Everglades Escape
Held for Ransom

Visit the Author Profile page at Harlequin.com.

HELD FOR RANSOM

KATHLEEN TAILER

LOVE INSPIRED SUSPENSE
INSPIRATIONAL ROMANCE

LOVE INSPIRED® SUSPENSE
INSPIRATIONAL ROMANCE

ISBN-13: 978-1-335-72250-8

Held for Ransom

Copyright © 2021 by Kathleen Tailer

Recycling programs for this product may not exist in your area.

This edition published by arrangement with Harlequin Books S.A.

For questions and comments about the quality of this book, please contact us at CustomerService@Harlequin.com.

Love Inspired
22 Adelaide St. West, 40th Floor
Toronto, Ontario M5H 4E3, Canada
www.Harlequin.com

Printed in U.S.A.

Fear thou not; for I am with thee: be not dismayed;
for I am thy God: I will strengthen thee;
yea, I will help thee; yea, I will uphold thee
with the right hand of my righteousness.
—*Isaiah* 41:10

For all of my neighbors in Oyster Bay and Shell Point who have blessed us immensely with their kindness, warmth and friendliness. May God bless you!

And, as always, for my wonderful and ever-growing family: Jim, James, Sophia, Bethany, Daniel, Keandra, Joshua O., Bradley, Jessica, Rachel, Nathan, Joshua E., Anna and Megan.

ONE

"I just kidnapped your sister."

The voice was metallic and distorted, yet still managed to send chills down Sophia Archer's spine, causing her entire body to tremble. She faltered and leaned against her car door for support. An image of her little sister, Kylie, in front of the dorm at her university, a big smile on her face, flitted through Sophia's mind. She nervously adjusted her cell phone against her ear. "What? Who is this? Is this some sort of joke?"

"My name doesn't matter, and this is no joke."

Sophia swallowed hard. "Is she okay?"

"For now," the tinny voice responded. "But she won't be for long if you don't do exactly what I say."

"I'll do whatever you want," Sophia said quickly, trying hard to keep from throwing up as fear clenched her stomach. "Just please don't hurt her. I don't have much money—"

"I don't want your money!" the hateful voice interrupted. "I want your investigative skills."

Sophia raised her eyebrow at the comment. She had been pleasantly surprised by the amount of notoriety she had gained as a reporter for the *Atlanta Times* during her recent exposé of an election fraud scandal. Her story had been the impetus for six arrests. What she hadn't expected, however, was the notoriety to hurt her or her family. If the caller wanted something investigated, why not just ask through normal channels?

The distorted voice continued as her thoughts churned. "Listen carefully, Ms. Archer. Go inside your apartment building. I've left a package by your door. Open it and you'll find further instructions inside. Follow those instructions to the letter or your sister dies. Got it?"

Despite the threat, a small defiant streak surfaced. "How do I know you really have my sister?"

"Kylie Archer, freshman studying English at Flint Rock University—right? Long brown hair, big brown eyes? Ring a bell?"

"So, you've seen her. That still doesn't mean you kidnapped her."

"I can send you one of her fingers if you'd like. Maybe the one wearing the high school ring from St. Mark's? The ring with the red stone in the middle over the treble clef?"

"No!" The nausea returned and Sophia swallowed convulsively. Her sister had played clarinet at St. Mark's high school, and that ring had been her pride and joy her senior year. She still wore it now, even in college. Sophia took a shaky breath. "Okay, but how do I know she's still alive?"

"You don't. You'll just have to wonder. But time isn't on your side, Ms. Archer. And if it turns out you don't care about your sister, I'm sure I can find another way to properly motivate you. Don't make me get creative. It won't just be you that pays the price. I'll go after every person involved in putting Arlo Prensky in prison, starting with that arresting officer. Just go open that package. I'll be in touch."

"Wait! Who is Arlo Prensky? What are you talking about?"

She heard a click. "Hello?" The kidnapper had disconnected. She pushed a few buttons, but nothing worked. The caller was listed as "unknown" anyway, and probably using a prepaid cell that would be impossible to track.

Sophia stowed her phone and shielded her eyes from the sun, glancing around her apartment building's parking lot as fear made her heart beat in her chest like a bass drum. No one seemed suspicious. Four cars over, a couple was walking hand in hand away from her. Across the lot, a woman was strapping her infant into a car seat, preparing to leave as she sang out loud to a song playing on the radio. Sophia didn't see a stranger stalking her, but that didn't mean someone wasn't watching from afar, observing her every move.

A jolt of electricity skidded down her spine, and her breath started coming in gasps as anxiety overwhelmed her. Was the abductor working alone or were there others? She glanced around again but saw no one suspicious. What did the kidnapper mean by threatening to *properly motivate her*? Were she and Kylie both going to be killed if the caller didn't get what was asked for?

Sophia took several deep breaths and tried to pull herself together, even though it seemed impossible. She had to focus. She had to think. She needed a plan.

She glanced at her watch as thoughts spun

and flittered in her mind. It was about ten in the morning, and the kidnapper had called just as she'd parked her car after returning from the gym. Did someone have a rifle trained on her now, prepared to shoot if she didn't immediately follow orders? She pulled out her phone and dialed Kylie, as she paced by her car. Hopefully, this entire episode was some sort of prank and Kylie was actually alive and well and just studying at her university library or reading her latest assignment at the duck pond where her classmates congregated.

Kylie's phone rang and rang. Sophia didn't leave a message, instead calling a second time, then a third. When there was still no answer, she ended the last call attempt, sent Kylie a frantic text, then crammed her phone back into her bag.

Her heart pounded as she turned and raced up the building's stairs to see if the kidnapper had actually left a box outside her door. She skidded to a stop in front of her second-floor apartment. A small shoebox, sealed with clear shipping tape, sat on her welcome mat. Her name and address had been written on the top on a bright blue label, but there was no postage and no return address. She stared at it for a moment as she tried to determine the safest course of action, but then the fear for her sister's safety took over. She quickly lifted the box and shook it gently, regardless of the possible danger, hoping it wasn't a bomb or some other dangerous device. On some level, Sophia knew she should call the police before opening the box, but she just couldn't wait—not with her sister's life hanging in the balance.

She hurried inside and dropped her gym bag on the couch as she made her way to her kitchen table. With shaky fingers, she grabbed a pair of scissors she kept in a kitchen drawer and quickly slit the tape. She held her breath as she removed the lid from the box. In the movies, the mysterious boxes never contained anything good…

This one contained newspaper clippings.

Surprised, she dug into the box with her fingers, feeling around the bottom, but there was nothing but paper. She pulled out the stack and started sifting through the pages. Each article, carefully trimmed around the edges, was in date order, the most recent on top. Some were paper-clipped together, where the continuation of the article had been printed on a different page. The clippings, she noted, were from a variety of state newspapers, and there were a couple from national sources. Each article was about the same person.

Arlo Prensky.

Just saying the man's name left a bitter taste in her mouth as the articles reminded her of the news stories she had seen splashed across the media only a few short months ago. She sank down into her kitchen chair and sorted through the headlines.

According to the most recent clipping, Arlo Prensky was currently on trial for the murder of a college student in the downtown Atlanta area. His victim, Maggie Spencer, had been a doctoral candidate at Atlanta State University. She'd been months away from earning her degree when her body had been discovered in a city park near the aquarium.

The clippings at the bottom of the pile detailed the search for the missing girl. The middle articles were about the murder and Arlo Prensky himself, identified by DNA found at the scene of the crime. The top clippings outlined Prensky's arrest and trial, and the defense attorney's failed attempts to change the venue to a location where the accused hadn't received such voluminous press coverage.

Sophia leaned back in her chair. What did this murder have to do with her or her sister? It just didn't make sense. She searched through the voluminous clippings more carefully, and this time came up with a small envelope wedged between a grouping. Sweat beaded on her forehead as she broke the seal, causing a photo to fall out. She noted the yellow piece of legal paper that was also inside the envelope but picked up the picture.

The image was of her sister. She was sitting in a chair with today's *Atlanta Times* propped against her feet so the date could easily be distinguished. Her hands and feet were tied with zip ties, and her mouth was gagged with a red bandanna. Her eyes, filled with tears, sent a silent plea for help.

Oh, Kylie.

Dear God, please protect my sister. Please keep her safe, and help me to do whatever it takes to make sure she survives this ordeal.

Sophia's eyes overflowed and she angrily wiped the tears away. Crying wouldn't help Kylie. Her anger couldn't push the fear away, though, and terror suddenly pulsed through Sophia as her ears started to ring. She couldn't lose Kylie. She just couldn't.

She closed her eyes, took a deep breath and

tried to settle herself. After a few moments, she swallowed hard and returned to studying the nondescript envelope. She pulled out the yellow paper that had accompanied the photo and started to read.

Arlo Prensky is innocent and I need you to prove it. If you want your sister to live, discover who the real killer is before the jury returns with its verdict. If you fail, you and your sister will die.

Sophia quickly turned her attention to the stack of clippings and found the one with information about the trial. The attorneys were to pick the jury today. She didn't know much about court hearings, but she doubted a murder trial would last longer than a week. She ignored the threat to herself and focused on the fact that Kylie had been kidnapped.

Her baby sister might only have days to live.

The enormity of the situation felt heavy on her shoulders. She said another prayer, this time asking for strength, and then stood, re-energized, and repacked everything in the box.

This was *not* a problem she could handle

on her own. She needed the police involved. Immediately. And she knew just who to contact, even though he was the last person on earth she actually wanted to see.

Sophia left her apartment, returned to her car and headed for the downtown Atlanta police station noted in one of the newspaper articles. At this point, nothing mattered but Kylie.

"You saw my picture where?" Noah Bradley asked as he leaned forward in his chair. He self-consciously wiped his palms on his pants and then anxiously flexed his fingers. He couldn't believe Sophia Archer sat across from him at his desk, or that he—by all accounts, one of the top detectives in the Atlanta Police Department—was suddenly so nervous.

Sophia motioned toward the package she had placed on his desk. "This box is full of articles from various newspapers. A couple of them highlight that you were the arresting officer in the Arlo Prensky case."

"That's correct. In fact, I'm scheduled to testify at his hearing tomorrow. What's your interest in the case?" Noah saw the stress lines around her mouth and eyes, and grimaced. He didn't know what was worrying her, but he felt a sudden urge to fix it.

Noah and Sophia had been neighbors growing up, and as children, they'd been inseparable. In high school, he'd developed a serious crush on Sophia, but when she'd ignored his advances, he'd stooped to playing tricks to salve his wounded pride and had ended up pushing her away. A troublemaker during his high school years, it had taken him quite a while to straighten out his life. When he'd finally settled on a career path, he'd joined law enforcement. He was still making amends to those he had hurt during those tumultuous times.

He shifted and wondered fleetingly if Sophia even remembered him with anything beyond disdain. He had been a total cad to her. He owned it. But her distracted mannerisms and anxious gestures made him think there was more to her anxiety than just hurt feelings and memories from the past. Her cheeks were flushed, and her beautiful brown eyes were rimmed with red. Something was definitely wrong. Something that went way beyond their shared history and the disastrous way he had destroyed their relationship. Her next words confirmed his suspicions.

"Look, Detective Bradley, I know it's been years since we've seen each other, and things didn't end well between us, but I'm desperate. I need your help. My sister has been kidnapped."

He straightened, suddenly all business. They could talk about the past later. "Kylie? Tell me what happened. Start at the beginning."

Sophia nodded. She then explained the details of the phone call, about the metallic-sounding voice and how she had found the box on her doorstep. Finally, she pulled out the envelope with the note and the picture of her sister that showed proof of life—at least, as of this morning. By the end of the tale, her eyes had welled with tears.

Noah didn't hesitate or think about what he was doing. He reached across the desk and covered her hands with his own, giving them a gentle squeeze. She flinched at his touch but allowed the contact for a moment before she pulled away. A few minutes later, her tears subsided and he fumbled in his desk until he found some clean napkins left over from the fast-food meal he had choked down for lunch the day before. He handed them to her, and she smiled gratefully, leaning away from him and wiping her eyes and nose.

"I'm sorry," she said sheepishly. "Our parents are gone, and all I have now is Kylie. I can't imagine what she's going through. I'm terrified that I'll never see her again."

"You don't need to apologize. I'd worry if you weren't upset." He pulled a pair of thin latex gloves out of his desk, snapped them on and opened the box, motioning to his partner, Charles Atwood, who was studying some documents at a nearby desk, as he did so.

"Hey, Charlie, can you drop whatever you're working on and come take a look at this? We've got a kidnapping, and every minute counts."

Charles nodded and quickly closed the file he had been reviewing. He joined Noah at his desk, listening with concern in his eyes as Noah brought him up to speed. He donned his own pair of gloves, letting Noah pepper Sophia with questions as they both riffled through the contents of the box.

"When was the last time you talked to your sister?"

Sophia hit a few buttons on her phone and found her call log. "February fifteenth, which was last Tuesday. She wanted to tell me her plans for spring break. I've been trying to reach her ever since I got that threatening phone call this morning and learned she'd been kidnapped, but her phone just goes to voice mail."

Noah nodded as he absorbed the information. "During your last call, did she sound worried or mention any people following her? You know, anything out of the ordinary?"

Sophia shook her head. "No, nothing like that. She was planning a beach trip with her friends. She was telling me that they wanted to drive down to Florida as a group. They had found a hotel, but they were still trying to work out the transportation issues."

"Do you or your sister have any connection to Arlo Prensky? Have you ever met him, worked with him…anything?" Charlie asked.

"No. Kylie's never mentioned him, and I've never met him. I really don't know anything about him that I haven't learned from the evening news or the paper. I haven't even had a chance to read through all of these clippings yet. Time is not on my side, Detective. Since jury selection has already started, I only have a couple of days to find out who really killed Maggie Spencer."

The two detectives finished sifting through

the contents of the box, Noah snapping pictures of each article and the photo and the note with his phone. Charlie put the contents back inside, grimacing as he put the picture of Kylie on top. He closed the lid. "I'll get this down to the lab. Hopefully, the perp left us a fingerprint or two. I'll have the lab make copies of everything inside so we can work through the contents without destroying any evidence. In the meantime, you can review the articles with the photos Noah just took with his phone."

Noah nodded and watched him leave for a moment before turning his attention back to Sophia. The pain he saw in her eyes made his heart clench. "I'm so sorry about Kylie. We'll do everything we can to save your sister, but you have to know that Arlo Prensky is guilty. There's no way you're going to be able to pin this on anybody else, especially not before the trial is over. We got the right guy, and that's exactly what I'm going to say tomorrow when I testify under oath."

Sophia swallowed and met his eyes. "I understand that, Detective, but I don't have a choice here. The kidnapper threatened to kill both Kylie and me if I didn't investigate this case. He also said he would start going after the people involved in Prensky's arrest if we didn't find the real killer. If you help me and we fail, your life could be in danger, too."

TWO

"I'm a police officer. I'm aware of the risks. But like I said, we've got the right guy, and that fact isn't going to change."

"Okay, Detective Bradley, but—"

"Call me Noah, please. We've known each other since we were three."

Sophia balled her fists as frustration swept over her. She should have known better. As soon as she found out Noah Bradley was the arresting officer, her heart had sunk clear to her toes. He had humiliated her in high school. In a few short years, he'd gone from being her best friend to her worst enemy, and she still didn't know why. She'd finally given up on him completely and hoped to never see him again, yet here she was, sitting at his desk and depending upon him for her sister's life. She swallowed hard, trying to get past the lump in her throat. Despite their shared history, she had to try to get his help, for Kylie's sake. Nothing was more important than Kylie.

Sophia bit her lip, then continued. "Noah, I need your help to rescue my sister and reinvestigate the Prensky case. You're probably a great detective, and I'm sure you and your team got the right man. Still, I don't have a choice here. The kidnapper is demanding that I prove Arlo Prensky is innocent, and I will do whatever I have to do to save my sister. If you won't help me, though, I'll do it myself."

Noah held up his hands in mock surrender. "Whoa, now. I didn't say I wouldn't help, and I apologize if I came across as defensive. As you saw, Charlie's already taken the box down to the lab, and he'll put a rush on getting the analysis completed since he knows time is of the essence. Those folks will analyze the photo, too, to see if there is any identifying information in there that can help us track down her location." He leaned forward. "Working with us is the best chance you have to get your sister back. All I meant earlier is that we got the right guy. Prensky is guilty. Nothing is going to change that fact." He motioned to another detective who was walking by. "Roman, I need you to set aside whatever you're working on. We've got a kidnapping."

"Absolutely," Roman answered, quickly giving them his full attention. He was a tall, broad-shouldered man, wearing an impeccably tailored dark suit with a red paisley tie and a very expensive pair of penny loafers. He didn't seem like a detective. Instead, he looked like he had just stepped out of a fashion magazine. Sophia wondered fleetingly if he focused on his work as much as he focused on his appearance. For Kylie's sake, she hoped so.

Noah turned to Sophia. "Roman is the best in the department at electronic tracking. Can you please give him your phone?"

Sophia quirked an eyebrow but complied, telling Roman her password as Noah gave him a brief overview of the case. The detective quickly turned on her phone, pushed several buttons and then nodded. "I'll be back in a moment. We'll put a trace on the phone in case the perp calls again, and we'll see if we can't figure out where the call came from in the first place."

He rushed off while Noah picked up his own phone. "Okay, if the kidnapper calls again, we'll go over every sound, every detail and every word of what the kidnapper says. Roman is also going to see if he can narrow down where the call originated. If there's anything there to find, he'll find it."

"I need that phone back," Sophia said, trying to keep the fear out of her voice. "When the kidnapper calls again, I need to answer my phone. I don't have a landline, and I don't plan on going home anyway or even sleeping until I meet the kidnapper's demands so Kylie'll be released."

Noah nodded. "You'll get it back. Just give Roman a few minutes to run the trace setup and download the data from your SIM card. I promise you, we are going to do everything we can to find her." He scribbled some notes on a small blue notepad. "What's the name of the college Kylie is attending?"

"Flint Rock University."

"That's about three hours south of here, right?"

Sophia nodded. Maybe Noah would help her after all. He seemed to be all business as he directed his team. Gone was the troublemaker she had known back in high school.

Sophia had to admit that he didn't even look like she remembered. She barely recognized him. He was wearing a dark suit with a light blue tie, and he seemed like a force to be reckoned with, even just sitting behind his desk. His dark hair was cut military-style, and he had filled out through the years, now broad and muscular. He exuded professionalism, and Sophia had to wonder how and why he had reformed. Had some horrible catalyst made him drastically change direction?

Before today, she'd pictured him with his long hair pulled back in a ponytail and holes in his jeans, riding his motorcycle around town as if he owned the world. She had never imagined that he'd even finish college, much less join law enforcement or earn the rank of detective. She was impressed, to say the least. Hopefully, that same drive and ambition he must have discovered somewhere along the way would help her find her sister before the abductor took her life.

"Tell me about her friends. Who does she hang out with down there?"

Sophia rattled off a few names, while Noah added to his notes. A few minutes later, Roman returned, handed her phone to her and then disappeared again. She turned back to Noah. When she finished listing Kylie's friends, he punched in a few numbers on his own phone and connected with Flint Rock University's campus police. He gave his credentials and asked them to open an investigation into Kylie's disappearance. Finally, after sharing his contact information and the details as he knew them, he ended the call and turned back to Sophia.

"That was Sergeant Kittinger I was speaking to. He seemed bright and motivated. He's going to start an investigation and interview her roommate and others who might know anything at all about Kylie's disappearance. He wants a copy of the photo of Kylie that the kidnapper put in the box, in case he might recognize something in the photo."

He texted Sergeant Kittinger the photo, then looked beyond her and motioned to someone. Sophia turned to see a large, balding, burly man in a gray suit talking to a uniformed officer on the other side of the room. The larger man made eye contact with Noah, nodded and waved him over.

She turned back to Noah as he said, "Give me a minute, Sophia. Then we'll pull out the Prensky file and I'll walk you through it." He stood and walked the twenty feet to the gray-suited man. After a quick conversation, Noah returned.

"Is that your boss?"

"Yes, he's my captain," Noah replied. "He'll make sure my other cases are covered while I work with you. Kylie comes first, especially since Prensky's jury selection started today. We don't want to waste even a minute. Timing is critical."

Sophia's heart tightened. She was overwhelmed with gratitude, despite the negative feelings she still harbored for Noah. "Thank you, Detective. You don't know how much this means to me. I really appreciate your help." She met his eyes and paused for a moment. Everything else about Noah might have changed, but his eyes were still a brilliant blue, the color of the ocean on a hot summer day. Where they had mocked her in the past, now she saw only respect and integrity in their depths. The change was surprising, to say the least. Again she wondered about his past and what had made him decide to become a law enforcement officer. But she pushed away the questions. She even pushed aside the danger to herself. Right now, the only thing that mattered was Kylie.

"You're welcome." He held her gaze for a moment, but his look was hard to decipher. It could have been introspective. She just wasn't sure. He suddenly looked away and grabbed his keys. "All right, let's go."

"Where are we going first?"

"Atlanta State University. You want to go over the Prensky case, so I'll walk you through it and show you the crime scene, as well. I've been reviewing the case anyway since I'm scheduled to go to court tomorrow, so a lot of the details are already fresh in my mind. During the drive over, we'll call the prosecutor, let her know what's going on, to see if she can get a continuance. In the meantime, Charlie and Roman will let us know as soon as either of them finds anything. You can also look at the pictures of those newspaper articles and read through them. I'll forward you the pictures from my phone." He gave her a tight smile. "You're an investigative reporter, for the *Times*, right?"

Sophia nodded. "Yes. How'd you know that?"

Noah shrugged. "I've seen one or two of your articles over the years. You did a great job on that election fraud case. A lot of people were talking about it."

He'd seen her work? She was surprised he would have even read it once he'd noticed her byline. "I thought you hated me, Noah. Why would you read any of my articles?"

A look of utter disbelief crossed his features. A look that he quickly masked. "I never hated you, Sophia. Never. Let's go." He held the door open for her, and she left the squad room with him right behind her. She could smell his clean, spicy aftershave—and another scent that reminded her of their childhood.

"You still chew Doublemint gum?"

He grinned. "You remembered?"

"Yes. If I'd known you were going to stick with the habit, I would have bought stock in the company." She smiled, but it quickly turned to a frown. "Tell me she's going to make it, Noah. Promise me Kylie is still alive and I'm going to see her again." She tried to keep her voice from shaking, but it just wasn't possible.

Noah shook his head. "I can't promise you that. What I can promise you is that I'm going to do everything I can to help you get her back safely."

Sophia thought he hated her? Good grief! They made their way to the university in relative silence as she read through the Prensky clippings, but he had stolen several looks at his passenger as they'd made the trip. He couldn't believe Sophia Archer was actually sitting in his car with him. Question after question filled his mind as he drove, but he said nothing and focused on the job at hand. Hopefully, there would be time later to re-hash the past.

He parked near the university's science building. As they got out of the car and headed for the front entrance, Noah's senses went on high alert, just in case. Once inside the building, he relaxed somewhat and lightly touched Sophia's back to guide her to the chemistry department. He felt her flinch at the contact and immediately dropped his hand as if he'd been burned.

He'd been a jerk to her in high school. It was his own fault that she was reacting this way. Despite what he had done and how he had treated her, however, he had loved Sophia back then. Even after she'd pushed him away, the love had burned within him. Her rejection had devastated his pride, and as a result, he had truly made a mess of things. But now that Sophia was back in his life for a few days, maybe God was giving him a second chance to make things right and earn her forgiveness. He wasn't going to waste it. He doubted she would ever come to care for him, but maybe he could at least make up for the past and they could part ways as friends once this was over.

Noah's mind turned to the case before them. Despite his reassurances, he was reluctant to reopen the Prensky file, especially since he didn't want anything to derail the trial. He had moved on to work other cases, but the details of Maggie Spencer's murder had stayed with him, given it had been a particularly heinous and needless homicide. Some cases were like that. Maggie Spencer had just been beginning her life. She'd had a bright future ahead of her.

Noah was confident Arlo Prensky was guilty of the murder and had taken great satisfaction in the arrest. But if taking another look would save Kylie and help Sophia absolve him of his past behavior, then he would do whatever it took to earn that redemption, especially since Sophia's life was in danger, as well. She had told him of the caller's threats, and it certainly seemed like the kidnapper was desperate and eager to ensure her cooperation. Had the abductor sent the driver in the black sedan to follow them? Was the perp prepared to follow through and start killing off anyone involved in the investigation if Prensky wasn't exonerated?

Noah led Sophia to the elevator inside the building, double-checked the directory and then headed toward the professors' offices. He'd called Maggie Spencer's professor on the way over to make the appointment to see him, but it had been a while since he'd been at the university and Noah didn't want to waste time going to the wrong place.

He sneaked a quick look at Sophia as the elevator rose. She was even more beautiful now than she had been back when they were teenagers. Her shoulder-length brown hair was cut in an attractive style that made her look both professional and feminine, and the sun caught the red highlights whenever she shook her head. Long lashes accentuated her large brown eyes. Her high cheekbones and porcelain skin made her classic looks even more appealing. Her body was full and shapely, and she was toned as if she played a sport or spent a lot of time at the gym. She had been a competitive swimmer back in high school. He wondered if she still swam for enjoyment.

He paused in his contemplations. Others might not find her as attractive as he did. They might say her smile was a little too wide or her determination to succeed made her appear a bit too fierce. But to him, she was simply magnificent. There had been no one else he had ever loved; only faint imitations at best. Yet even so, after all that had passed between them, he knew it was impossible they'd ever end up together.

Focus. He had to stay focused. Sophia and her sister were victims who, after he solved this case, would return to their separate lives. Forgiveness was the best he could realistically hope for.

But forgiveness would be worth it.

THREE

"Tell me again where we are going?" Sophia asked, breaking into Noah's train of thought.

He shook his head as he came back into the present. "I wanted you to meet Professor Keenan. Maggie Spencer, the victim, was his research assistant. She was working with him on her dissertation when she died. She was just a few months away from her graduation. Her old office is in this building, too, but it's in the basement. The university promised to leave it untouched until the trial ended. We can go there after we talk to the professor so you can take a look and see where she worked."

Professor Reginald Keenan met them at his office door. He was a short, thin-haired man with a brown goatee sprinkled with gray and sharp, penetrating brown eyes behind wire-rimmed glasses. He appeared strong and brawny beneath his tweed jacket and dark brown pleated pants, yet also studious and refined. Noah guessed his age to be late fifties or early sixties, though noted his face was lined with stress marks that likely made him look older than he actually was.

The professor shook hands with both of them as Noah introduced Sophia, and Noah noticed that his hands were clammy, despite the firm handshake. Keenan motioned them into his office, toward two leather chairs positioned in front of his desk, then took his own seat across from them. "Security alerted me that you were on the way up. Is there something I should know about the trial?"

Noah shook his head as he and Sophia took the proffered chairs. As he sat, the height of the chair surprised him. It was closer to the ground than most chairs, causing him to look up at Keenan, whose own chair was significantly higher. Noah shifted. He had never particularly liked Professor Keenan, who had always seemed convinced that he was the smartest person in the room. The setup of the office and the shorter chairs just solidified that dislike. "Ms. Archer works with the *Times*, and she's interested in the Spencer case. Since you and I will both be testifying, I thought it couldn't hurt to go over the details of Ms. Spencer's murder with her since we have to review the facts anyway to prepare for our testimony."

Keenan steepled his fingers and gave them both a direct look. "I'm not sure what I can tell you that I haven't discussed already. This seems rather like a waste of time, and I am a very busy man."

"Well, Professor, Detective Bradley told me you were the expert on the case, but if you feel like you can't contribute..."

Keenan put up his hands. "I didn't say that." He leaned back. "Ask your questions."

Noah smiled to himself. Sophia had read the man perfectly and had played to his vanity to gain his cooperation. By all accounts, she was a very successful reporter, and he enjoyed seeing her in action, despite the circumstances.

"How well did you know Ms. Spencer? I mean, I realize she was your research assistant, but exactly what did that entail?"

"We worked together on several projects during the last two years and met nearly every day to discuss the status of the various issues that arose. I was supervising her work on her dissertation, as well. She was a bright girl, but she needed quite a bit of guidance."

"Were you friends outside of work? Ever have dinner together or go out socially?"

Keenan narrowed his eyes. "Absolutely not."

"Tell me about the day she disappeared." Sophia didn't miss a beat. Noah noticed she had taken out her phone and was making notes on a special app. She appeared totally unruffled by the professor's hard demeanor.

"Ms. Spencer was actually a bit upset that day. She had made some mistakes on one of my research projects, and I'd had to correct her and put her on the right track. She argued with me, vehemently, but finally saw the wisdom in my advice. She told me she was going to start fresh the next day. As you probably already know, that was the last time I saw her. It was around 5:30 p.m. I don't know where she went after she left my office."

"Besides being frustrated about her work, did she say anything else that concerned you? Like she'd had an argument with a boyfriend, or something like that?"

"Ms. Archer, have you ever worked on a doctoral degree?" His tone had a bit of a sneer to it, but to Sophia's credit, she didn't react.

"No, sir."

"My research assistants don't have time for anything beyond chemistry, believe me, and Ms. Spencer's work was suffering lately. She surely didn't have time for a boyfriend or a social life. We had even decided to postpone the defense of her dissertation. Her work had been substandard, and she needed to refocus her energies."

This was news to Noah. He wondered why Professor Keenan had never mentioned that about her dissertation before. Noah leaned forward. "If you had to guess, why was she distracted?"

"Financial difficulties, I presume," the professor answered. "She was distraught about staying in school another semester and wasn't sure how she was going to pay for it."

"Was she in danger of losing her scholarships?" Sophia pressed.

Keenan's eyes narrowed. "I do not work for the financial aid department, Ms. Archer. You'll have to ask them."

"Well, would she have remained your research assistant if she had stayed another semester?"

Keenan shrugged. "That hadn't been determined."

"Even if she wasn't dating, did she ever

mention any problems with anyone?" Sophia asked. "A fight with a roommate, an argument with a friend?"

"Not to me. We talked about chemistry and chemistry alone. Our relationship was purely professional."

Sophia nodded, finished writing her notes and stood. "You've been very helpful, Professor. We really appreciate your time. If you think of anything else that might be pertinent, please don't hesitate to contact Detective Bradley."

"Yes, of course."

"Before we leave, we'd like to take a look at her office, if you don't mind?" Noah said, standing, as well. He was glad the interview had been short. His legs were cramping from being at such an awkward angle in the little chair. Being six-two and nearly sitting on the floor was not a comfortable proposition.

Keenan stood. "Be my guest. Detective, I imagine I'll see you in court." He nodded. "Ms. Archer, it was a pleasure meeting you. Thanks for stopping by."

Noah and Sophia exited the room and Keenan closed his office door firmly behind them.

"Feel like we've been dismissed?" Noah whispered.

* * *

Sophia cringed. "What a pompous, arrogant man," she whispered back. "I can't imagine working for him day in and day out." They turned and headed back to the elevator.

"Me, either. I didn't even like interviewing him during the initial investigation, but he did tell me something new today that he'd never mentioned before—Maggie was going to have to come back for another semester, and her assistantship was in jeopardy. That must have been devastating news to her, especially if she was having financial problems. I'm not sure how it fits into this case since her murder seemed like a crime of opportunity rather than something premeditated, but still, it's interesting that he never mentioned it before."

Sophia's thoughts swirled as she contemplated what she had just learned. Unfortunately, her ruminations only brought up more questions. "How was she supporting herself if her whole life revolved around chemistry? She must have been paid a stipend or something for her research work, but it couldn't have been much."

"She was earning about thirty thousand a year as Keenan's assistant, and she was taking out loans to pay her school costs. She'd had some pretty heavy debt waiting for her once she graduated. It's a common theme I've seen before. People get the loans to go to school, and then their entry-level salaries barely cover the costs of repayment and a tiny little apartment."

Noah's phone rang right as they stepped out of the basement-level elevator, and he motioned for Sophia to wait. "Hold on. I need to take this." He said hello and then told the caller he was switching to speakerphone so Sophia could hear. "Go ahead, Sergeant Kittinger. Kylie's sister, Sophia Archer, is here with me."

"I just wanted to touch base and give you my preliminary report. I've spoken to Kylie's roommate and interviewed some of her friends. She was last seen around 7:00 a.m. this morning. Last night, she had dinner in the cafeteria, worked in the library until around 10:00 p.m., spoke to a few people and then went to her dorm. Nothing out of the ordinary happened.

"This morning, she got up and had breakfast in her room, then grabbed her backpack and headed to class at around 8:30 a.m. Her roommate was the last person to speak to her. The class is a large one, and no one I've talked to can confirm whether or not she attended."

Sophia's eyes welled with tears.

Noah took her hand and squeezed it gently in a motion of support, then released it.

She felt so powerless. She hated the feeling and pushed it away, letting determination take its place.

"Thanks for the report, Sergeant. Please continue searching and keep us informed. We're investigating on this end, as well, and I'll let you know if we get any leads."

"Copy that. We're doing everything we can to find her." Both men hung up, and Noah stowed his phone. He turned to Sophia. "Are you okay?" When she nodded, he motioned toward a hallway. "Let's go see Maggie's desk."

They followed a maze of corridors until they came to a nondescript door propped open with the broken end of a broom handle. There was a tag with a room number, but no window, names or other information about what the room contained.

Sophia glanced around the office. "Isn't it a bit strange that this building is so empty?

We haven't seen a single student down here in the basement or in the hallways."

Noah shrugged. "It's quieter than I remember, but this floor never had many people around during the investigation. Maybe all the students are in class. And graduate assistants aren't given the primo offices. They're lucky to even have desks in the building, especially if the other professors share Keenan's view of their worth. It's probably par for the course to keep them tucked away in the basement and out of sight."

Despite Noah's words, Sophia thought it was strange that research assistants weren't housed closer to their professors' offices. This particular room held four desks, each occupied by one of the science graduates. There was another room nearby that held another group of four. According to the nameplates on the desks, only one of the remaining graduate assistants who shared this office worked in the chemistry department. The rest were assigned to different disciplines.

"I've interviewed the other three that shared this office, and none remembered seeing her the night she disappeared," Noah said in a matter-of-fact tone. "As best as we can tell, Maggie met with Professor Keenan, came down here to grab a few things and then left. Security has her leaving the building alone around 6:00 p.m. Her body was discovered in the park around 11:00 p.m., and the coroner estimated that her time of death was between 9:00 and 10:00 p.m. We think she was walking in the park, and Arlo Prensky saw the opportunity to rob her and took advantage of it."

Sophia walked over to the desk surrounded by yellow crime tape. "Was anything missing from her desk?"

"Nothing anyone noticed."

"What about her phone?"

"We never found it. We figured she had it with her in the park, and it was stolen by the perp. We did get a list of her calls, though, and we didn't see any red flags."

"What about her laptop?"

"We never found that or the blue hard drive her roommate claimed she used instead of cloud storage. We assume she had both with her in her computer bag, as well."

Sophia frowned. "So how do you know what she was working on?"

Noah shrugged. "Professor Keenan gave us a thumb drive with her latest projects. We had them analyzed. Nothing seemed out of the ordinary."

"Did she normally walk through the park with her laptop at night?" Sophia asked.

"Apparently, she liked to walk, and the park was one of her favorite places to go. Her roommate said walking helped her clear her head. It makes sense that she'd want to walk off some steam after her argument with Professor Keenan. She must have been so upset that she didn't think to store her computer somewhere safe before she left. Her laptop was fairly new, and it was an expensive lightweight model with a lot of bells and whistles. We checked the pawnshops and other outlets where we hoped the computer might show up, but it was never recovered. We searched for it at Prensky's residence, too, but like I said, we never found it."

Sophia absorbed the information as she studied the items on Maggie's desk. "Is it okay for me to touch a few things?"

"Sure. Go ahead."

She opened a few files and then started going through the drawers. She raised her head and turned as footsteps sounded outside the doorway. "Finally, another live person. I was beginning to wonder if anyone else ever came in this building."

Strangely, the footsteps started running, and then suddenly there was a loud bang as the broomstick was removed and the heavy metal office door slammed closed. Noah put his hand on his pistol, motioned for Sophia to stay behind him and walked cautiously over to the door.

Abruptly, more loud noises sounded from outside the door, as if someone was hammering. A sense of dread washed over Sophia as Noah pushed against the door. Fear sent tingles down her arms and legs, and it was suddenly hard for her to breathe.

The door wouldn't budge. They were locked inside. And it was no accident.

FOUR

"We're locked in?" Sophia asked, surprised. Noah nodded, and she felt a ball of panic start to rise in her throat. She swallowed hard. They couldn't be stuck in here. She already had precious little time to investigate this case, and every passing minute without answers kept Kylie's life—and her own—in jeopardy. She joined Noah at the door and studied it critically. The hinges were on the outside, and she couldn't see any way to force it open from the inside. There was also no window in the door, so it was impossible to know what was going on in the hallway, if anything. The loud noises had stopped; they heard nothing but silence now.

Noah pushed against the handle, but the door didn't budge. He dropped to the floor and tried to look underneath it. But the large rubber seal attached to the outside blocked his view. "The door isn't locked, but it won't open. It looks like someone hammered wedges under the door and around the sides to keep it from opening. Somebody definitely wants us to stay in this room. The questions are, why and for how long?" He pulled out his cell phone, and Sophia did the same as she felt the panic start to rise in her chest.

"I don't have a signal. Do you?" she asked, hoping the anxiety wasn't making her voice sound as desperate to him as it sounded to her own ears.

Noah shook his head. "Nope. This is probably a really bad area." He pocketed his phone and glanced around the room. "There's not a single landline in here, either."

Sophia's mouth went dry as a sense of desperation overtook her. She swallowed, hard. How was she going to find Kylie's kidnapper if she was locked in this room? Even losing a few hours could put her sister's life in jeopardy. She went over to the nearest desktop computer and pushed a few keys. It jumped to life but the screen immediately asked for a password.

"It's protected. I imagine all of these will be." She went to the next desk and tried that one, then to the third. Riffling through the contents of the various desks yielded nothing of value, either. She was hoping to find a password scribbled under a keyboard or taped to a drawer in one of the desks, but she found nothing that would help. A thought suddenly hit her. "Was Maggie's computer taken for evidence?"

"Yes, but apparently she rarely used the desktop except to access a few university databases. She worked primarily on that missing laptop."

Sophia's hands started shaking. She couldn't stop them. She ran the few steps that it took to get to the door and started pushing against it. Nothing happened. She took a few steps back and then threw her entire body into it, trying to force it to open. It didn't move.

Noah held up his hands. "Whoa. Keep that up and all you're going to get is a sore shoulder. That door won't budge."

She looked up at Noah but slammed her body against the door once again anyway. She had to get out of there. Now. When she moved to shove it again, he got in the way, gently took her arms and held her steady. "Please don't. That's not going to help. You're wasting your time, and you really are going to hurt yourself."

"You don't understand!" She pulled away from him and started hitting the door with her fists, hoping to make enough noise that someone would come. She could feel the panic taking over and she was helpless to stop it. "I have to get out of here. Kylie's life is in my hands!"

"No, Kylie's life is in God's hands. And we don't have to waste the time in here. We can talk about the case and run through the details until something pops. Meanwhile, the lab is doing its job, and Charlie, Roman and Sergeant Kittinger down at Flint Rock are all trying to find out where Kylie is and who's responsible. The investigation will continue even if we're not at the helm, I promise you."

He took her hands again. "I don't think banging on that door is going to help, either. We're way at the end of the hallway, and as you've already noticed, there aren't a lot of people in this part of the building to hear you. My team will realize I'm missing pretty soon, though, and they'll come looking. They knew we were heading over here."

She pulled away again and started pacing. He was right. Her shoulder did hurt. But he still didn't seem to understand the danger. "Look, Noah, the man who took Kylie threatened my life—and yours, too. There could be a bomb in the building or—"

He held up his hands again, and his tone was soft and calming. "Let's use the time to talk through the case, not worry about possibilities," he suggested. "Who would want to keep us prisoner in here? It doesn't make sense. The person that sent you the box *wanted* you to investigate. It's counterintuitive."

"I agree," she said, matching his tone. She was grateful for his quiet demeanor. Without it, she would positively be going nuts right now. She pulled aside the yellow crime tape and sat in Maggie's chair.

Noah was right. If she had to be stuck here, she could at least make good use of the time. Methodically, she sorted through the contents in and around the desk. There was the normal variety of office supplies, several folders filled with chemistry formulas and notes, and several reference books, a few with library slips sticking out the top, showing they were due on various dates. "There's not much here. Most of her research and work must have been on that missing laptop and hard drive."

Noah nodded. "We sorted through the desk

like you are doing today and didn't find anything out of the ordinary. We double-checked
the cloud, as well, and we didn't find any accounts or files registered to her on the sites
her roommate suggested. Of course, without
the laptop, it's hard to know which sites she
visited on a regular basis and which projects
occupied the majority of her time. The desktop computer was linked to the library, and
it seemed like she used that machine mostly
for work email and for research and checking citations."

Sophia's forehead wrinkled in thought.
"What about the files Keenan provided?"

"The work was bare-bones, and all seemed
rather mundane. Nothing that pointed to murder, anyway. The emails also revolved around
chemistry and work assignments. We didn't
find any smoking guns." He paused momentarily. "The crime seems to be one of opportunity, like I said before. Maggie was walking
through the park and had an expensive laptop
with her. Arlo Prensky killed her and then
robbed her. It was a crime of opportunity."

Sophia stowed the folders back where she
had found them and then turned to face Noah,
who was sitting at a nearby desk. "Was there

any connection between Prensky and Maggie before the murder?"

"None that we found. Prensky had been involved in some studies that were being conducted at the Atlanta State medical school, so it's possible that they bumped into each other on campus, but that's the only connection we found. There's no record of Maggie and Prensky ever meeting or being involved with the same project at any time."

"What kind of studies?" Sophia asked.

"Some sort of medical research. Prensky was basically a lab rat, and he received some cash for participating. It had something to do with medication side effects, or something like that. I think they were testing a new medication for diabetes, but I couldn't get many details because of the health privacy laws. Maggie hadn't been involved with the tests in any way, though, so we didn't pursue it. We didn't find a single link between the perpetrator and the victim."

Sophia stood and started pacing again. She was going to go crazy if she didn't figure something out soon. All she could think about was her poor sister, scared and at the mercy of some criminal. The image from the picture the kidnapper had sent kept flitting through her mind. She was afraid that vision would be burned into her brain forever. She had to do something, anything, to get out of this room.

She pulled out her cell phone and walked around the entire room, checking to see if the signal improved as she moved. Nothing. Not even one bar showed on her screen. Once again, panic began to tighten in her chest. Her sister would be dead soon, and there wasn't a single thing she could do about it.

Sophia started to pray.

An idea suddenly hit her and she started checking the outlets in the room to see exactly what was drawing power in the office. There was a power strip behind each desk where the computer, monitor and printers were plugged in. A couple of the grad students had desk lamps that were also plugged into the power bars, as well as other devices. She knelt by the wad of cords and then, one by one, followed each cord with her hand to determine what was connected to what.

"What are you looking for?" Noah asked.

"I did a story a while back about a prison near Albany, Georgia, that was using cell jammers to keep prisoners from using illegal phones. Evidently, someone was smuggling the phones in and it became a huge problem that the prison couldn't control. Of course, cell jammers are illegal in the US, so that was also a problem, and the prison warden got in a lot of trouble for using them."

Noah raised an eyebrow. "You think someone is jamming our signal?"

Sophia shrugged and twirled the ring on her finger in a nervous gesture. "It's a possibility. Somebody locked us in here for a reason. It makes sense that if they'd go to the trouble of hammering wedges around the door, they would have a plan in place to keep us from calling for help, as well."

She brushed some dust off her navy pants. "Installing one down here really isn't as crazy as it sounds. According to my research, a couple of universities were toying with the idea of using jammers during exams. Apparently, because some students use cell phones to cheat, the problem became so pervasive that the schools in question considered drastic measures. I don't think the idea was ever approved anywhere, though. Cell phone signals are all regulated by the feds, and they rarely allow anyone to block the signals because, in times of emergency, important calls still need to get through. The universities would have had to get special permission to use one."

"Was Atlanta State one of those universities that tried to get permission?" Noah asked.

"I really don't remember. It's been a while since I did the research."

"So, you think someone knew we were coming today and purposefully put a cell jammer in this room?"

Sophia shrugged. "It's possible. It's also possible that if we find a jammer, it has absolutely nothing to do with us. Maybe one of the professors put one down here to keep the graduate students off their phones and focused on their studies. Or one of the students could have set one up to harass a graduate assistant. The possibilities are endless."

Noah put his hands on his hips. "I've heard of cell phone jammers, but I've never seen one. Do you know what they look like?"

"They're about the size of a deck of cards—" Sophia made a square with her hands "—and have a few antennae sticking out, kind of like your average modem. They can be battery-powered, but I imagine if there is one in this room, it's plugged into the wall somewhere. Otherwise, the owner would have to keep coming down here to check the batteries, and that might be suspicious." She moved to the next desk and repeated the process of checking all the outlets.

Noah nodded, intrigued by the information. If they could get a signal, they could call for help and be rescued even sooner. "I'll help you look."

While Sophia checked all the power strips around the desks, he moved to the outside walls of the room, searching for outlets. He started near the door and moved a filing cabinet to check behind it, glad to have something to do. He was a man of action; sitting around waiting for something to happen had always been difficult for him. Especially now, when a young girl's life was being held in the balance.

He glanced back at Sophia, who had moved on to the next power bar. She was one smart cookie. He had always admired her for that.

His thoughts moved to Prensky and the case before them. He had been so sure they had arrested the right man for Maggie Spencer's murder, but their current predicament had started a niggling pain in his gut. Someone didn't like the fact that they were reopening the investigation. It was the only reason that someone would try to sideline them. But why? Why lock them in the basement at the university if not to slow them down and hinder their progress?

Thankfully, if they couldn't escape, his disappearance would be noted at the trial tomorrow, if not sooner, and the police would start searching for him. His partner, Charlie, could testify in court just as easily. Though Noah's name was on the report as the primary arresting officer, the event had been a joint effort. There were other officers who could testify, if needed. The trial would continue with or without him.

So, if someone wasn't trying to stop the trial and keep him from testifying, then what was going on? The only thing that made sense was that someone didn't want them asking questions and exonerating Arlo Prensky. But why? Noah was convinced the man was guilty. They could investigate until the cows came home and it wouldn't change the outcome. What did it hurt to retrace the facts to confirm the results?

And how had anyone even found out? Only a handful of people knew what he and Sophia were doing, and Prensky was days away from a lengthy prison sentence.

Noah paused a moment, thinking through the possibilities as the questions ate at him.

"Found it!" Sophia declared triumphantly, breaking into his train of thought.

She turned to Noah and held up a small device with four black-rubber-coated antennae sticking out of the top. A power cord extended from the back of the device to the power strip, the small green light on the front showing that the power was on.

Noah came over to get a closer look. "Good grief! This does look like a modem. Even if I had seen it sitting on a desk, I would have never guessed it was anything else. And what's even more interesting is that it's kind of dusty. Someone didn't just pull this out of the box recently and set it up in here. It's been here awhile."

Sophia met his eyes. Hers were filled with questions.

"I don't know what it means," he said quickly, before she could ask the question forming in both of their minds. "But someone wanted to make sure that once we were locked in, we weren't able to call for help."

FIVE

Sophia pulled the plug out of the power bar and the green light on the front of the jammer disappeared. "Now check your phone."

Noah did just that and couldn't stop the grin from spreading across his face. "Two bars. Looks like we're back in business." He immediately dialed his office. "Charlie, we need help." He explained what had happened and where they were located, then hung up and stored his phone. "They're on the way. It shouldn't be long now."

Sophia breathed a noticeable sigh of relief, pulled up one of the office chairs and sat. "I just can't figure this out. Whoever put that cell phone jammer down here could get arrested, or at a minimum, get fined and thrown out of the university. Why would anyone want to take that chance? It's not like the grad students are privy to secret information that's going to change the world."

"That's an excellent question, but I have a feeling that if we ask Keenan and the other professors who have assistants down here, they'll all act surprised and won't tell us the truth. Like you said, nobody is going to admit to breaking the law."

Sophia nodded. "I agree. We need to talk to one or more of the other grad students who shared this office with Maggie. It might have nothing to do with Maggie's murder, but then again, it would be good to get the insight, just in case. And," she added with a thoughtful look, "if we can figure out who put the jammer in here, it might lead us to whoever locked us in here." She leaned back in her chair. "Tell me more about the night Maggie died."

Noah pulled up his own chair. "Well, like I said, she met with Keenan, then came to her office and presumably packed up what she was planning to take home, including her laptop. She left the building and went on a walk in the park across the street. She was probably on the sidewalk that led to the fountain on the eastern side when she was attacked.

"Prensky came up behind her and hit her

head with a rock. She was stunned, but she fought back and was able to scratch him pretty deeply on the arms and face. The medical examiner said the initial head wound would have made Maggie dizzy, and it was probably hard for her to struggle, but she gave it her best shot. We found Prensky's DNA at the crime scene and under Maggie's fingernails.

"Apparently, he hit her twice more on the head before she fell forward and didn't get up again. She died from the blunt force trauma. Prensky tried to hide her body behind some bushes and dragged it about twenty feet from where the incident occurred. Her computer and phone were never recovered."

Noah noticed Sophia shiver. "Sorry. It's such a horrible story. Maggie Spencer was in the prime of her life. We don't think it was premeditated, and thankfully, she wasn't sexually assaulted. She just happened to be in the wrong place at the wrong time. Prensky saw the opportunity and took advantage of it."

Sophia looked up and her eyes were filled with tears. Noah wanted to comfort her, but knew instinctively that she would not welcome his touch. "How horrible," she said softly. She reached for a tissue from a box on the nearby desk and wiped her eyes. "Tell me about Arlo Prensky. Did anyone see him kill Maggie Spencer?"

"No, there weren't any witnesses. But, like I said, his DNA was all over the crime scene. Plus, he didn't have an alibi."

"No alibi at all?"

"Nothing that we could prove. He claimed he went out drinking, then went home and passed out. A few people said he had been at the bar, and they stated he left around 9:00 p.m. That gave him plenty of time to kill Maggie and go home. No one saw him for the rest of the evening."

Sophia twisted the ring on her finger again. Noah realized she probably didn't even know she was doing it. "I'm guessing he was pretty scratched up?"

"Yes, he had scratches on his face and arms, and of course he couldn't remember how he had gotten them. He was still pretty out of it when we arrested him the next morning."

"Was he having financial trouble?"

Noah shifted. "Yes. In fact, his finances were so bad that he was about to be evicted. He hadn't paid his rent in three months. That's why he was helping with the ASU medical study, too. All the participants were paid a fee for their services, but it wasn't very much. Prensky needed money, and he needed it fast. We're fairly certain money was the motive. Prensky had already served five years in prison for drug dealing and theft. He was no stranger to crime, and since he had a prior theft charge, we figured he knew who to contact to fence the stolen property. He lived about two miles from the university in a seedier part of Atlanta. We found cocaine in his apartment, although he claimed it wasn't his. He had a part-time job as a clerk at a convenience store and…" He stood suddenly. "Do you smell that?"

Sophia sniffed the air. "Smell what?"

"I think I smell gas."

Sophia's face showed her alarm. "Gas? Are you sure?"

Noah sniffed again and looked hurriedly around the room. His eyes zeroed in on the pipes bolted to the ceiling from one end of the room to the other. He couldn't see any visible damage, but the smell was rapidly increasing. "I think one of those pipes might be leaking, unless the gas is entering through one of the air vents." He quickly dialed 9-1-1 to report the leak, and then he called Charlie to tell him what to expect when his team arrived.

Sophia put her hand over her mouth and nose, then pulled up her shirt to cover her face. "I smell it now. What do we do? There's no way out of this room!"

Noah dropped to the floor and motioned for her to join him. "Stay as low as possible. Let's get nearer to the door so that the second help arrives, we'll be able to get some fresh air."

They crawled toward the door, but about ten feet from their destination, Sophia collapsed, overcome by the fumes.

Noah pulled off his jacket and covered Sophia's face with it. He then put his arm solicitously around her, hoping to protect her until the experts arrived. He heard shouting from the other side of the door, but was unable to call out. His last conscious thought was that someone didn't just want them out of the way during Prensky's trial.

Someone wanted them dead.

The pounding in her head wouldn't stop.

Sophia pulled the pillow closer, hoping for some relief.

"Sophia?"

She moved the pillow and listened. She knew she had a headache, but she quickly realized that the pounding sounds weren't coming from her dreams. They were coming from Noah, who was knocking on her bedroom door.

Noah was in her apartment?

Oh, yeah. Yesterday. Kylie. Gas leak. Reality came crashing in and she sat up, a bit too fast, and then moaned as the pain in her head intensified. Normally, she would feel strange about having a man in her apartment, and even stranger about having him see her before she'd had a chance to shower and get her act together in the morning.

But this was Noah, who'd known her most of her life. This was Noah, who knew what she looked like without makeup and without her hair combed. The situation she found herself in also changed her focus. She would let just about anyone see her morning face and hair if it would help her discover Kylie's whereabouts. This was no time for vanity. And Noah was here to help. He was here as a friend, and he had changed. She had to remember that.

"Noah? Come on in."

The doorknob turned and he stuck his head around the door, a tentative smile on his face.

"You okay? You said you wanted to get an early start, but it's already eight thirty."

Sophia glanced at the clock by her bed and groaned. "Yeah, sorry. I've got a horrible headache."

Noah frowned. "Sorry about that. I made some breakfast. Will that help?"

"It might." She rubbed her forehead. "Give me five minutes."

"Done." Noah softly closed the door, and Sophia leaned back against her pillow and massaged her temples. The doctor had told her that a headache was one of the symptoms she would feel as a result of the inhalation injury she had sustained in the university basement. According to the team in the ER, she was experiencing an inflammatory reaction to the gas she had breathed, which was also causing a tightness in her chest. Thankfully, the doctor had said the symptoms would only last a week or so, and he'd claimed that over-the-counter pain meds would take away the bulk of the symptoms. Then she should be back to normal. She grimaced. The doctor had also told her to drink plenty of fluids and get lots of rest, but "lots of rest" wasn't going to happen.

She had to free her sister.

Sophia pushed the covers aside and made her way to the bathroom and the medicine cabinet. A few minutes later, she headed for the kitchen, where she could hear Noah rustling around. As she passed it, she glanced at the sofa where he had spent the night, noting he'd already folded the blankets and stacked them neatly with the pillow on top.

Noah Bradley was in her apartment.

If someone had told her even a few days ago that this was a possibility, she would have laughed herself silly. But now everything had changed.

After the attempt on their lives at the university, Noah had insisted on staying with her to make sure she was safe. He had tried to talk her into going to a hotel and getting adjoining rooms, but she had refused outright. She wanted to be in her own apartment. He'd only backed off when she had finally agreed to let him sleep on her couch so he could make sure she'd be safe. She hadn't wanted to inconvenience him either way, but he had been very persistent after they'd been discharged from the hospital. In the end, she just hadn't been up for an argument.

"You made waffles?" she asked when she saw the breakfast spread. She couldn't keep the surprise from her voice. Somehow, he'd managed to put a gourmet meal together on her kitchen counter. He'd made a fruit salad, juiced her oranges, baked three waffles and sautéed some ham slices with fresh pineapple. Coffee simmered in the pot behind him, adding to the wonderful smells that were filling up her nostrils.

Who was this man? she asked herself. He was nothing like she remembered.

Noah shrugged and failed to hide his smile. "Breakfast is the most important meal of the day. I want you to have a fresh start."

"You didn't need to go to so much trouble."

"I wanted to. And it was no trouble. I like spending time in the kitchen, and I like cooking for you."

Sophia still couldn't believe that Noah was standing in her kitchen, spatula in hand, and they were having a normal conversation. Yet there he stood, looking incredibly pleased with himself for surprising her.

She studied him surreptitiously as she took a plate and filled it. He was wearing a new gray suit, which he apparently kept in his car for times when he didn't make it home. His navy tie accented the sea-blue color of his eyes. His chiseled cheekbones and strong chin complemented his law enforcement persona to a tee, and his brow was expressive as it flashed between compassion and determination, depending upon the need.

He'd also brought a toiletry bag in from his car, but he'd been so busy cooking he hadn't yet had time to shave. She was secretly glad, particularly since she found the dark shadow on his face roguishly appealing. She had to admit he had grown into one good-looking man. Yet even so, whenever she looked at him, she felt conflicted. He was helping her now, yet it was so hard to forget the past and erase the hurt he had caused.

In high school, after she had repeatedly refused to go out with him, he had started playing embarrassing tricks on her and derailing her studies. The pranks had been harmless enough in the beginning.

He'd once had a pizza delivered to her in her homeroom class. He'd also had roses sent to her swim class complete with a singing telegram. A month later, he'd filled her locker with Ping-Pong balls so that when she opened it, the balls bounced all over the hallway. He'd stuffed her car with balloons and then wrapped it in Saran Wrap. When that hadn't triggered a rise from her, and she still refused his advances, the tricks had turned from harmless fun to humiliation.

She'd finally had enough when he'd put peanut butter under her car door handles and Vaseline on her windshield wipers. The sticky mess on her hands had been bad enough, but the petroleum jelly on her windshield had made it so hard to see that she'd almost had an accident before she'd been able to pull over and clean it all off.

She'd confronted him after the incident, but he'd been totally unrepentant. In fact, he had teased her about her driving in front of a large group of their classmates. For weeks afterward, she found jars of peanut butter and petroleum jelly everywhere she went. On her desk. In her gym locker. In her backpack. Kids could be cruel in high school, and the comments had turned offensive and nasty as the school year went on. She had become the butt of countless jokes, and Noah had joined in and egged others on. His words had been the most painful of all.

Now Sophia looked into his sea-blue eyes and saw caring and kindness in his expression, not the rowdy teenager that she remembered. She wasn't interested in a relationship with the man, but maybe it was time to put the past in the past and to let go of the pain he had caused her. After all, they were adults now. Could they actually be friends again? She wondered if such a thing was even possible.

They sat at the kitchen table and, after a short prayer, dug into the fabulous breakfast he had prepared.

"This is wonderful of you. You really didn't have to do all this," she said softly after taking a few bites.

Noah shrugged. "I wanted to. We didn't get here until two this morning, and I wanted to give you a chance to rest a little longer before we headed out. You can't help Kylie if you wear yourself out."

"Well, thank you." She took a sip of her juice. "Are you feeling okay after yesterday? You breathed that gas, too."

He nodded. "My throat hurts a little, and I'm a bit tired, but it will pass." He poured some syrup on his waffle. "I want to start at the park today to show you the crime scene, since we didn't get to do that yesterday. I have to be at the courthouse at eleven, but before that, we can also check in with everybody and see what the lab found." He took a bite, chewed and swallowed. "I just talked to Sergeant Kittinger at Flint Rock a little while ago. He didn't have anything new to report, but he said he is pursuing the investigation at top speed and his whole team is searching for Kylie. He claims finding her is his number one priority."

She raised her eyebrow. "*Claims?* That's a funny word to use. You don't believe him?"

Noah paused before taking another bite. "I'm not sure. He seems sincere, but there was something about his voice... It's probably nothing. Just my suspicious nature mixing with that gas attack in the basement yesterday. That was definitely no accident. Someone tampered with the gas lines leading into that room after locking us in."

"Who had access?"

He shrugged. "Just about anybody. The detectives found the door unlocked. They checked for fingerprints but didn't find any. Whoever damaged the lines probably wore gloves."

Sophia put down her fork. "It sounds like someone wants to stop us from reinvestigating. Should we go to Flint Rock and look for Kylie instead of trying to free Prensky? I've been wondering all along if we shouldn't have started with trying to find her instead of looking into the case again, but I was hoping that by complying with the kidnapper's demands, Kylie would stand a better chance of surviving this mess."

"I think we should keep working on the case here in Atlanta, like we planned. Sergeant Kittinger is handling the Flint Rock investigation, and it's clear the kidnapper is watching you—or has somebody watching you. I saw a suspicious car following us on our way over to the university yesterday, and last night, I noticed a woman at the hospital who gave me some concern. She disappeared before I could confront her, though. Even if both events were innocent, until we know more, it makes sense to focus on the kidnapper's demands so it appears like we're complying."

Sophia frowned and sat back in her chair. "You didn't want to tell me about the car or the woman at the hospital earlier? That seems like pretty important information. I thought we were working this case together."

"We are," Noah quickly assured her. He apparently noticed her expression and back-pedaled. "I'm sorry. You're right—I should have told you sooner. I just didn't want to make you any more worried than you already were, but now I see that I was wrong. From here on in, if I see something that concerns me, I'll share it. I promise." He nodded toward her fork. "You really need to eat more. You'll need your strength to investigate this case, and Kylie would want you to take care of yourself."

Mollified, Sophia let him change the subject. She wanted to argue further, but he had already apologized, and there was nothing more to say. She also knew that he was right about eating a good breakfast. It wouldn't do any of them any good if she didn't get proper rest and nourishment, even though the last thing she felt like doing was sitting down to a meal. She felt a touch of nausea, but wasn't sure if it was a result of her lung injury or her worry for her sister. Still, she pushed the feelings aside and ate what she could. She finished quickly, then put the leftovers in the fridge, dressed for the day in gray slacks and a navy button-down shirt, and met Noah by the door. She glanced at her watch. Nine fifteen.

Hopefully, before this day was over, Kylie would be safely home, ready to complete her spring break plans, and this nightmare would be behind her.

SIX

"Detective, who murdered Maggie Spencer?" The attorney stopped right in front of Noah, making sure he could clearly see and point to the defendant. The lawyer's body language punctuated her words.

"Arlo Prensky. He's the man in the navy jacket, sitting at the defense's table."

The prosecutor turned and looked over at the jury, slowly making eye contact with each of them, giving them all time to absorb Noah's words. "Your Honor, please have the record reflect that Detective Bradley is pointing to Arlo Prensky, the defendant."

"It will so reflect."

The attorney continued. "And why are you so sure that you have arrested the correct perpetrator?"

Sophia leaned a bit to the left so she could have a good view of the jury. They were all watching Noah closely as he testified, and they were genuinely hanging on his every word. She glanced back up at Noah from her seat near the back of the courtroom. She had to admit, he exuded authority.

After breakfast, they'd gone over to the crime scene and walked through what the police had discovered, and then come straight to the court for him to testify. There hadn't been much to see at the park anyway—no longer an active crime scene, the yellow crime tape had been removed long ago. Still, just knowing a young woman had lost her life at that spot had moved them both.

Sophia watched as Noah continued, his voice grim.

"We found Mr. Prensky's DNA at the scene. Ms. Spencer fought back against her attacker and scratched his arms and hands. When we arrested Mr. Prensky, he had matching scratches on his hands and arms. We also found Mr. Prensky's blood on Ms. Spencer's legs from where he'd grabbed her ankles to drag her body after the murder. Blood was also on Ms. Spencer's head near the wounds she sustained and under her fingernails, along with skin cells from the scratches."

"And how do you know it was Mr. Prensky's DNA you found at the crime scene?"

"The medical examiner tested the DNA, matched it to Mr. Prensky's DNA already in the system and reported the match to our office."

A murmur arose through the gallery as members of the audience commented among themselves while the prosecutor crossed back to her table and picked up a document. "I'm showing the court the medical examiner's report previously accepted into evidence as the state's Exhibit A-5."

"No objection," the defense attorney stated in a monotone voice.

"Is this the report you are referring to?" the prosecutor asked, showing him the report.

"Yes, that's the one," Noah replied.

"Did you interview Mr. Prensky?"

"Yes. After the arrest, we performed several interviews."

"How many is 'several,' Detective?"

"We spoke to Mr. Prensky on four separate occasions."

"And during those four occasions, did Mr. Prensky ever provide an alibi for the time in question?"

Sophia looked over at Prensky, who spent

his time smiling at his supporters and glaring at Noah from the defense's table. The man had a look of pure hatred in his eyes, the anger seeming to radiate from him in waves as Noah testified.

"He claimed to be at home alone, but we couldn't find anyone to corroborate that."

"He was home alone!" a voice suddenly yelled from the gallery of the courtroom. A man stood and fisted his hand above his head. He was large, had an overgrown beard, dark, unfriendly eyes, and his hair was pulled back in an unruly ponytail. He was wearing jeans and a faded T-shirt that proclaimed Sal's Pizza was the best in the Atlanta metro area. There was a large stain near the left shoulder. Sophia didn't recognize him, but his facial features proclaimed a biological relationship to the defendant. Was he a brother? A cousin? She couldn't tell.

"You have the wrong man!" the man continued. "He doesn't need an alibi because he's innocent!"

"That's right!" another man agreed. He stood and added his voice to the stained-shirt pizza lover standing next to him. This man was older than the first, but although he was better dressed and wearing new jeans and a white dress shirt, the anger and frustration in his eyes matched the first man's expression. "Prensky is innocent!"

"Order!" the judge said loudly as he banged his gavel. "Gentlemen, you will both sit down and be quiet or you will leave the courtroom."

"How can I sit here and watch you railroad an innocent man?" the first man asked.

The bailiff reached the first protester, took him by the arm and started leading him toward the exit at the back of the room. The man took one step, then another, before pulling his arm free and turning back to the . judge.

"Arlo Prensky is innocent!" he yelled again. This time his voice was joined by a chorus of several others in the gallery who were sitting behind Arlo's defense table. Three women stood and joined the two men, and soon they were all shaking their fists and yelling at the judge. Next, two young men stood and joined the fray, as well.

"You'll be sorry you lied!" one yelled at Noah, pointing his finger at him. "I'll teach you not to lie!"

"Yeah, you'll be sorry!" another joined in.

A cacophony of shouting and shuffling ensued as five new bailiffs entered the courtroom from the hallway and started trying to calm the crowd. A grin split Arlo's face as his supporters yelled at the judge, the witness and the bailiffs. Handcuffs came out, and it took the law enforcement officers a good ten minutes to remove the protesters and bring the room back under control. Only the man in the white shirt and a couple of the other Prensky supporters were left once the bailiffs were finished, and the judge admonished the remaining few with a short speech full of reproach.

Finally, the prosecutor was able to repeat her question and continue the trial. "Detective Bradley, did Mr. Prensky have an alibi for the night Maggie Spencer was murdered?"

"He claimed he was home alone."

"And was he?"

"We couldn't confirm his whereabouts—except for the fact that his DNA was found on Ms. Spencer's body."

"No more questions," the prosecutor stated as she went back and sat behind her table.

The defense attorney stood and approached Noah, who was still sitting in the witness stand. "Officer Bradley…"

"I'm a detective," Noah corrected.

"Ah, that's right. Okay. Detective Bradley…" he droned, his voice holding a touch of mockery.

"When you questioned Mr. Prensky, did he tell you why he had those marks on his hands and arms?"

Noah nodded. "He claimed that he had been working on a landscape job and sustained the injuries working with plants."

"Did anyone he did landscape work with corroborate that explanation for his injuries?"

"We talked to his supervisor, who confirmed he had been working with roses and palm trees."

"Could those plants have caused the scratches on my client's arms and hands?"

"Sure," Noah agreed. He turned to the jury and made eye contact with them once again. When he spoke, his words were succinct. "But like I said before, that can't explain why Mr. Prensky's DNA was at the crime scene or on Ms. Spencer's body."

"Did you see that man?" Sophia demanded as soon as they had left the courtroom and the door closed behind them. Her eyes were spitting fire and had turned a golden brown as the anger consumed her.

Noah took her arm and gently led her away

from the courtroom entrance so their voices wouldn't disturb anyone. "Who? There were lots of men in there. And women."

He'd been surprised by the number of people watching the trial. The majority of them seemed to be university students from Atlanta State, based on their clothing and youth, but the gallery had held a fair share of Prensky's personal supporters, as well. Since most criminal trials were open to the public in Georgia, and this case had been well publicized, maybe Noah shouldn't have been so surprised.

He had also seen a woman seated on Prensky's side of the courtroom whom he'd recognized from the hospital. He was sure of it now—the woman was definitely following them. She had been one of the people the bailiff had removed during his testimony, though, so she was probably long gone. He glanced around surreptitiously and confirmed that she was not among the bystanders milling around the doors to the courtroom. He should tell Sophia, but once again, he hesitated. She had so much on her plate already, and he really hated to heap on more stress and anxiety.

He dragged his hand through his hair and

took a deep breath, glad that his part of the trial was over. He wasn't a big fan of testifying. He preferred the investigative duty of his job, but it was all part and parcel of the same goal: putting away the bad guys and getting them off the streets before they hurt anybody else.

During his testimony, he'd seen Maggie's parents in the gallery, as well. They'd been sitting in the first row, right behind the prosecutor's table, their hands tightly linked as the evidence of Maggie's last days on earth played out in front of them. It had been Noah's job to deliver the death notice to them as the lead case investigator. That was not an easy chore, and it was definitely one aspect of his job that he truly hated. He knew that after he told a victim's family the news, their lives would never again be the same. Now, at this stage of the case, it had been hard to watch them suffer even further as they'd listened to the details that emerged during the trial.

He stopped his woolgathering and turned his attention back to Sophia. "What did the man you saw look like?"

She glanced over his shoulder as if trying to spot the man in the hallway, but when she saw there were only a few people milling around, she turned back to him. The people who had disrupted the trial had undoubtedly been escorted from the building, but he thought she was probably still checking to make sure she was safe.

"He was about six feet tall, with sandy brown hair that's graying at the temples and hazel eyes. Midfifties, if I had to guess. He had a small scar on his cheek here." She drew her finger down her cheek on the right side. "And he was wearing jeans and a white button-down shirt."

"I'm sorry, but I really didn't notice him. I was concentrating on my testimony. What about him?"

"He was staring at me the entire time I was sitting in the gallery. I… I think he had something to do with Kylie's kidnapping."

"Kylie's kidnapping? What made you suspect him? Did he say anything to you?" Noah asked.

Sophia shook her head, but her body was still rigid with stress and adrenaline. "No, but he gave me the creeps. He was clearly on Prensky's side for the trial. He didn't stand up and yell like the others, but he thinks Prensky is innocent. I could see it in the way he reacted to your testimony. Hatred was shooting from his eyes. That man is dangerous!"

She leaned closer and kept her voice low. "And who else but someone involved with the kidnapping would know who I am? I'm not famous. I'm not a TV reporter, and I've never done a story on this case. He would have no reason to recognize me or to even notice me unless he had something to do with Kylie's disappearance. I could be wrong, but I really think we need to talk to him."

Noah hadn't noticed the man Sophia had described, but it made sense that whoever had kidnapped Kylie was someone from Prensky's family or a friend who was willing to go to any extreme to free him. It also made sense that the kidnapper, or someone working with the perp, would attend the trial. Sergeant Kittinger and his team were supposed to be looking for connections between Kylie and Prensky, but so far, they hadn't found any. Still, if the man Sophia was describing had reacted to her presence at the trial, there was a good chance he knew something about what had happened to Kylie. It was definitely worth finding out more.

"You're right. Let's go." They walked over to where the bailiff was standing by the door, and Noah pulled out his badge and introduced himself. "We need to speak to a gentleman sitting in the gallery wearing jeans and a white dress shirt. He has graying brown hair, a scar on his cheek, and is probably in his midfifties. Can you bring him out for us?"

The bailiff nodded. "Happy to help, Detective. Where was he sitting?"

"On the defense's side, about midway back, near the aisle. We have a few questions for him."

The bailiff nodded. "You got it. Give me a minute." He went into the courtroom and came back out a moment later, followed by the man Sophia had described. The man immediately looked Sophia and Noah over from top to bottom and narrowed his eyes. He held himself as if he was barely able to contain his anger.

"What do you want?" he snapped, derision in his voice.

"There's a place at the end of the hallway where you can talk," the bailiff said huskily, pointing to the left. Putting one hand on his hip and the other on the butt of his holstered gun, he rocked back and forth on the balls of his feet. As he gave the man a silent warning to cooperate, it was clear he would tolerate no more monkey business in his courtroom.

"We just have a few questions, sir. Do you mind?" Noah said, his voice carefully cordial. He motioned with his arm toward the area the bailiff had suggested.

The man blew out a breath. "As long as it doesn't take too long. I have to get back into the trial. I don't want to miss anything important."

The three of them walked about thirty feet to where the hallway ended in a small alcove. Noah pulled his badge out of his pocket and showed it to the man. "I'm Detective Bradley with the Atlanta Police Department, and this is Sophia Archer."

"I know who you are. I heard your testimony." He glanced at Sophia but quickly moved his eyes back. "Ask your questions."

Noah pressed his lips into a thin line. "First, can I see your identification, please?"

The man grumbled under his breath, but he pulled his wallet out of his pocket. He produced a Georgia driver's license and handed it over. "What's this about, anyway?"

Noah took the license and compared the photo to the man standing in front of him. It was the same person. The ID read John

Prensky and provided an address of a small suburb south of Atlanta. "Mr. Prensky, can you please tell me how you're related to the defendant in this case?"

The man frowned and his lip curled. "I don't need to tell you anything."

"And I don't need to let you back in that courtroom, either. We can finish this conversation back at my office downtown. The choice is yours."

Prensky glared at the two of them but finally relented. "Arlo is my sister's boy. She's been dead for a while now, so I look out for him from time to time."

That explained the resemblance. This man, however, was neat in appearance and didn't seem nearly as rough around the edges as some of Prensky's other relatives. "I don't remember talking to you during the investigation," Noah said in a tone that clearly asked for an explanation.

"That's because I was out of town when Arlo was arrested. You would have heard from me if I'd been here." Prensky glanced at his watch. "Anything else? I need to get back to the trial."

If he wasn't in town, then it was doubtful that he had any information vital to Arlo's case, but that didn't mean he didn't know something about Kylie's disappearance. "I'd like to know why you were staring at my friend here," Noah said, motioning to Sophia.

Prensky shrugged. "No reason. I was looking at a lot of people."

"But you were staring at *her*."

The man glanced at his watch again. "I didn't mean anything by it. I don't know this woman, but she looks similar to a friend of mine. Once I got a better look, I realized she wasn't my friend after all. Now, if it's okay with you, I'm ready to go back in the courtroom. I want to hear every single word of the testimony. You all are trying to railroad my nephew, and I don't appreciate it. Is there anything else?"

Noah glanced over at Sophia with a question in his eyes, but she shook her head, almost imperceptibly, and he looked back at Prensky. He handed the man back his driver's license. They would need to do a background check to find out more before they could question John Prensky further. Staring at someone was creepy, but it wasn't illegal. "No, sir. Thank you for your time."

The man pocketed his ID and quickly hurried back to the courtroom door, where he nodded at the bailiff as he entered.

"He knows something," Sophia said tightly under her breath.

"He might," Noah responded. "His behavior is a bit suspicious, and if he's involved with Kylie's kidnapping, it makes sense that he would be keeping an eye on you to see if you are complying with his demands." He shifted from one foot to the other as the possibilities swam in his head. Then his eyes locked with Sophia's. "It's time to make some calls. We need a status report from each of the officers before we go anywhere, and I'll ask Roman to start checking into John Prensky immediately."

SEVEN

The two walked even farther away from the courtroom so they could have a little privacy as they figured out their next move. Sophia watched Noah as he spoke on the phone, and a wave of emotion hit her that was so strong it nearly knocked her to her knees. Time was passing. Her sister's life was in danger, and she had never felt so hopeless and afraid. The feelings only intensified as she watched Noah. His body language showed that he was also frustrated and not encouraged by what he was learning on his calls.

She looked fleetingly around the narrow hallway. Seeing a bench against the wall, she went over and sat. It was time to pray. She needed God's help more than ever; she needed His intervention and His strength. She closed her eyes and spent several moments alone with the Lord. After a few minutes, she felt Noah come over and sit beside her, but she kept her eyes closed, deep in contemplation.

Noah took her hand and held it. Instead of pulling away, she allowed the contact, grateful for his support. After a few more minutes passed, he put his arm around her shoulders and pulled her close. She allowed that, too, leaning into his strength. He was warm and she liked the way she fit against him. She felt safe, like everything was going to be okay, and he smelled minty and fresh, like his Doublemint gum, which calmed her even further.

Finally, she turned and looked into his eyes. She saw confidence and caring in those depths, and a touch of something else she couldn't quite define. She had to admit, she was glad he was there, helping her, doing everything in his power to support her.

And it was costing him, too. She wasn't blind to that fact. Noah had investigated, arrested and even testified against Arlo Prensky. He was convinced of his guilt. Yet Noah was still with her, spending countless hours reinvestigating everything, questioning all of his prior work and conclusions on this case, all to help her save her sister. She was touched by his sacrifice, moved by this side of him she had never really seen before.

"Thank you for helping me," she said softly. "I realize this isn't easy for you."

He gave her a gentle smile. "I would do anything for you."

She looked deeper into his caring blue eyes and saw the truth behind his words, even though she wasn't ready to really think about the implications of that simple statement. His look was mesmerizing. She touched his face softly with her fingertips, then dropped her hand, surprised at her own reaction. This wasn't the time or place to think of anything beyond her sister's fate. She pulled back, ready to refocus. "What did you find out with your calls?"

Noah leaned back, too, but he left his arm across the back of the bench, remaining in contact. The look in his eyes was unreadable. "Well, I talked to the lab. Our perp must have done everything with gloves on because there were no prints found besides yours on the box or on any of the contents. The materials and notepaper found inside are too common to trace. I checked in with Roman about your phone, but unfortunately, the kidnapper's call can't be tracked. Probably used a burner phone."

Sophia took a deep breath. "So now what do we do?"

"I've asked Charlie and Roman to work together to investigate who might have taken Kylie. They had both already started, but they were going down different paths. I want them to compare notes. Since we don't have any leads, it makes sense to assume someone close to Prensky is pulling the strings. My guess is a family member or close friend—maybe even a girlfriend—is behind the kidnapping. They're the ones with a vested interest in his release. After what just happened, I asked them to start with John Prensky." He met her eyes again. "The prosecutor plans on resting her case this afternoon. That means the defense will start presenting its case first thing in the morning."

Sophia shook her head. "We're running out of time."

"Yes, but I'm not giving up."

"Neither am I."

Noah paused and pursed his lips. "I saw a woman here today that I'd seen before. She was one of the people who got thrown out of the courtroom for yelling when Prensky's relatives went crazy during my testimony." He ran his hand through his hair. "She's gone now, so we can't talk to her, but I'm pretty sure she was at the hospital last night."

"Was she working there?" Sophia said hopefully.

"No, and I don't think she's the only one who has been following us. I don't have any proof, but my gut tells me we're being surveyed."

"What should we do?"

"Stay vigilant," he replied. "We already think the kidnapper has people watching to make sure you are really investigating Prensky's case, but somebody else wants to stop the investigation. What we don't know is how many people are involved. We need to keep our eyes wide open."

They both stood.

"I'm thinking we should interview Maggie's roommate again. Maybe she can share something new with us. At least it is worth a try," Noah said as he motioned toward the hallway. "Ready?"

"Sure. Let's go."

They left the courthouse and headed to the parking deck where they had left their car, an unmarked silver sedan.

After driving only a couple of blocks, Sophia noticed a car coming up closely behind them. She sat straighter and took another look. "Do you see that blue sedan? I think it's following us."

Noah glanced in his rearview mirror as he changed lanes. "Yes, I see it, but that's not the same car that was following us before. Let's see if it wants to stick with us." The blue sedan disappeared for a few blocks, but soon showed up behind them only a short while later.

"He's back," Sophia said, trying to keep the panic from her voice. "Can you see who's driving?"

Noah shook his head, his eyes moving between the road and the car that was following them. "Whoever it is, they're wearing a hoodie and glasses. I'm guessing it's a male, by the size of the driver, but it's really hard to tell." He pulled out his phone and called for backup, then quickly dropped his phone into his shirt pocket and swerved into another lane.

Sophia grabbed her armrest and held on tightly. "This can't be the same person who kidnapped Kylie."

"No, this is different," Noah agreed, his voice tense. "The others only seemed to be following us to make sure we were complying with the kidnapper's demands, but this guy is driving aggressively. He's trying to cause an accident. Keep your eyes open in case he has a gun or some other weapon, and hold on. It looks like somebody wants us to stop investigating and apparently is willing to go to any lengths to make sure we do."

Sophia cried out as the blue automobile drew closer and then slammed them hard from behind. Noah struggled with the wheel but kept control, neatly avoiding crashing into a green pickup and a white minivan parked alongside the road. Other drivers, aware of the hostile attacker, tried to get out of the way, but the Atlanta traffic was heavy and there were few places for most of them to go to avoid the mayhem.

The blue car driver's erratic behavior became even more threatening, and smoke appeared as the vehicle's wheels spun against the pavement. The assailant accelerated once again, pulling up inches behind them before slamming into their trunk a second time. They both cried out as Noah pulled hard against the wheel, fighting to keep the vehicle in the lane. Suddenly the assailant hit a pothole and momentarily lost control. A horrible squeal sounded and the blue car fishtailed into a black truck on the other side of the road. A loud crash followed and a larger cloud of smoke soared into the sky. Metal screeched against metal as another vehicle hit the blue automobile, sending it farther into the thoroughfare. The sedan slowed— the driver's-side fender and door now quite damaged—but the determined driver didn't stop the pursuit. Instead, he punched the engine and, in a matter of moments, was able to sweep up behind Noah and ram them once again.

Sirens sounded in the background, but all Sophia could think of was the driver of the blue sedan, who was now striking a third time, trying to force their car off the road and into the row of parked cars that lined the street. She felt Noah accelerate, but their small-engine car was no match for the larger older-model blue sedan. Her fingers turned white against the armrest as she dug into the vinyl. Her other hand gripped the seat belt as fear consumed her. Was she going to die today, right here and now, without ever seeing Kylie again?

Noah saw an opening as a side road appeared to the right, and he veered in, turning sharply as the tires whined in protest. He accelerated, once again hoping to put some distance between their car and their pursuer's. The blue automobile missed the turn but took another side street and was quickly behind them in only a matter of seconds. Suddenly, Noah heard a gunshot, and his rear windshield shattered. Bits of glass and debris went flying in all directions, and he heard Sophia scream behind him.

"Get down!" Noah yelled as he struggled with the wheel. He wanted to help Sophia, but there was really nothing he could do other than keep the car on the road and as far away as possible from the shooter. Another bullet whizzed between them to crack the front windshield, and a third bullet hit the dash just above the radio. He ducked, but there wasn't really any place for him to go. If he stopped the car, they would both be killed. If he continued driving, he could have a horrible accident or unknowingly put them both directly in the line of fire. His choices were few and awful, no matter what he decided.

Noah pulled out his weapon and returned fire, trying to aim and keep his eye on the road at the same time, which was almost impossible. His first shot went wild, but his second shot did manage to hit the front headlight of the blue car. Still, his offensive gesture had the desired effect. The hooded man wasn't happy that Noah was shooting at him, and he dropped back about fifteen feet, giving Noah a little breathing room.

Noah turned and fired again, his third shot hitting the blue car on the passenger side. He took a deep breath, reduced his speed and then squeezed off a fourth round, paying careful attention to his aim, while also hoping that no one pulled out in front of him. Their pursuer's passenger's-side tire exploded and the blue sedan swerved dangerously. It flipped and skidded about thirty feet to a crashing stop into the side of a parked white Prius.

Noah did a fast pull-over, stopped his car with a jerk and turned off the engine. He reached out and grabbed Sophia's hand, catching her eye as she looked toward him. "Are you okay?"

She nodded but didn't say a word. Terror was clearly etched across her face. Her eyes were wild.

"Stay down and stay in the car," he soothed. "I have to check the driver."

She nodded her agreement and he squeezed her hand in response, then unhooked his seat belt and pushed open the door, staying low as he got out of the vehicle. He didn't know if their attacker was even alive or still in his car, but he had to check. He kept his 9 mm at the ready, his aim steady on the blue sedan. The airbag had deployed, and as he got closer, Noah could see that the driver was still in his seat, his blood smeared against the bag and what was left of the side window. He was injured and moaning.

"Throw the gun out the window now!" Noah ordered as he approached the vehicle from the rear, carefully eyeing the man's movements.

"I dropped it." The man's voice was barely audible. "I lost it when the car flipped. I don't know where it is."

Noah didn't trust him and kept his weapon trained on the driver, regardless of his claims. He cautiously came up to the driver's-side door and noticed that the man was still held in place by the car's seat belt, even though the automobile was resting on its roof. "Put your hands out the window where I can see them."

The driver groaned but complied. Blood trickled down his hands, which were shaking as he held them out the window, his fingers held wide apart. Noah still approached cautiously, but was able to handcuff the driver without incident. He smelled gasoline and saw a river of the noxious liquid flowing under the car. He needed to get them both far away from the overturned sedan as soon as possible.

"Keep your hands where I can see them," Noah ordered. He looked through the windows and noticed a gun on the roof near the back seat. He opened the rear door, secured the attacker's gun and his own, then opened the driver's door and helped the man out and away from the damaged vehicle.

Once he was seated on the curb, Noah pulled off the attacker's hood and glasses, and looked him over from head to toe. He had green eyes, dark hair, and was probably in his early thirties. Noah racked his brain, but didn't recognize him.

"What's your name?" he asked as he quickly checked him for other weapons. He found none.

The man shrugged and looked away, obviously uncooperative. Nathan pulled out his phone and snapped his picture, then tried again. "You want to tell me why you tried to kill me and my passenger?" He moved to stand in the man's line of vision, but once again, the attacker turned his head, not willing to engage.

Another police car arrived, and two officers approached, guns drawn.

"I'm Detective Bradley from the two-nine. The perp is disarmed but injured," Noah announced to the new arrivals. "Can you call a bus?" he asked the closest officer, using the police vernacular for an ambulance. The woman nodded and made the call while the other officer kept his gun trained on the perpetrator.

Noah ordered both officers to keep an eye on him as he quickly went back to the blue sedan and searched it. He didn't know how long he had before that leaking gasoline caused a problem. He found some paperwork in the glove box that showed the car as registered to a female. He shuffled through some other items, but found nothing to give him any insight into the man's identity or what was going on.

The car, he realized, had likely been stolen. But why was the driver trying to kill them? Had someone sent him or had he been working on his own? How was this guy involved, if at all, in the Arlo Prensky case?

Noah had been on the job as a detective for

a few years now, and he had racked up his fair share of enemies, but his instincts told him this guy was somehow connected to Prensky, especially since he'd been tailing them once they'd left the courthouse. However, if the guy wouldn't talk, finding answers to these questions was going to slow their investigation even further, and they had precious little time already to save Kylie Archer.

He pulled out his phone and called Charlie. He brought his partner up to speed about what had happened, then asked, "Any news about Kylie?"

"None," Charlie confirmed. "And we're getting static from Kittinger in Flint Rock. I think we're going to have to go down there ourselves to figure out what is going on. I'm heading out in about fifteen minutes."

The news surprised him. "Static? The sergeant seemed on board before, although I did have a feeling in my gut that something was off."

"Well, your gut was right," Charlie said, his tone acerbic. "We've called the local PD and had better success there. I'm not even convinced Kittinger was honest about his work on the case. Hopefully, the local boys have some connections to the campus police and can help us make some headway. Either way, it's slow going."

"What about John Prensky?"

"Nothing pops in his background. He's clean. He's a well-respected businessman with interests in a few different types of companies. It looks like he makes most of his money in real estate, but he also runs a couple of import businesses. No red flags or shady dealings."

Noah digested the information. Instead of advancing past square one, he felt like they were moving backward, and the entire time, Prensky's trial was proceeding on schedule, leaving them very little time to figure out where Kylie was being held.

"Okay, Charlie, I'm going to need some help. This perp isn't cooperating, and I need someone to process him and interview him while Sophia and I continue the investigation. We have to do whatever we can in the short time we have left." He paused and looked over at his vehicle, where Sophia was still ensconced in the front seat. "I'm also going to need a new car. Mine has pretty much been destroyed."

"Understood. I'll get Roman to do the interview, and I'll clear it with the boss so we can pull Matthews in. He just finished a drug case and can help us out. I'll also send some new wheels your way. You need to stay with Sophia and keep her safe. It's obvious she's a target."

Noah nodded, his muscles tense. "Thanks, Charlie. Tell Matthews I owe him one. And call me if anything breaks."

"You got it."

Noah hung up and ran his hands through his hair, his frustration causing a knot to form in his stomach. He always wanted to do his best and solve his cases, but this one was special. This one involved Sophia, and he wanted so badly to help her and to save her sister that it was tearing him up inside. He reached in his pocket and popped an antacid into his mouth instead of the gum he usually chose, then went back over to his damaged car and approached the passenger side.

Sophia opened the door and quickly got out, but she stayed by the side of the car. She motioned to the driver, who was still sitting on the curb where Noah had left him, guarded by the officer.

"Is he okay?"

"He's a bit banged up, but he'll live. How are you doing?"

She brushed aside the question. "I'm okay. Did he tell you who he was or why he was trying to kill us?"

Noah shook his head, his lips drawing into a thin line. "Not a word. I've got him set up to be interrogated when they clear him medically, but all of that is going to take time."

Sophia's eyes rounded. "But we don't have time…"

Noah put up his hands in mock surrender. "I know. Believe me. One of the other guys from my unit will do the interrogation to see if they can figure out his motive and whether or not he's connected. In the meantime, we need to head on over to Maggie's roommate's house. She was expecting us a while ago, so I'll call her in a minute to make sure she is still available."

He pulled out his phone again and showed Sophia a closer picture of the man who had tried to run them off the road. "Recognize him?"

She studied the photo carefully but finally shook her head. "No, but he might not have anything to do with the Prensky case, right?"

"It's possible," Noah allowed. "But I'm not ruling out anything until we know more."

Sophia handed him back his phone just

as another officer approached. "Detective, I understand you need some new wheels. You can take my car if you promise not to get it shot up." He gave a crooked smile and held up some keys. "It's the black one over there behind the tape." He pointed, and Noah followed the officer's motion to a newer-model sedan parked outside of the crime scene ribbon.

Noah gave him a smile and took the keys. "Thanks. I promise to try to keep it on the pavement and not fill it with too many new holes before I return it."

The officer laughed. "Yeah, we'll see how good you are at keeping your promises. I hear you drive in the demolition derby on the weekends. Good thing that car is insured." His voice turned serious. "I understand this is the second attempt on your life in twenty-four hours. You'd better watch your back."

"That's the plan. Thanks for the loaner." Noah motioned to Sophia. "Are you ready to go?"

"Ready," she answered, and the two of them started walking toward the new car.

EIGHT

It didn't take them too long to get to Maggie's old apartment. When they arrived, Joanna Crawley met them at the door and invited them inside. She was a rather short, rotund woman in her early thirties, and she had a wistful, innocent look in her eyes that made her seem approachable and friendly. She was average-looking and wore little makeup, with clear, smooth skin and dark brown eyes. But what stood out the most was her poise and bearing. Joanna was a woman clearly confident in her abilities and happy with her life, despite her humble surroundings. Sophia seemed to like her immediately, so Noah took a step back and let her take the lead.

"Thanks for waiting," Sophia said as she noticed Joanna's gym bag by the door. "Sorry to hold you back."

"It's not a problem. I just joined that gym

down the street. I wanted to take advantage of the membership, but I can go later." Joanna motioned them into the living room, where there was a couch and two chairs.

Noah noticed that the room was clean but decorated with inexpensive and mismatched furniture. The apartment smelled spicy, as if Joanna had been cooking Mexican food, and his stomach rumbled as he remembered he hadn't eaten much today. Maybe later he and Sophia could grab something at a fast-food restaurant.

Their hostess sat in one of the chairs and waited for them both to take a seat before voicing her questions. "I'm not sure why you're here. I mean, I want to help because I cared about Maggie, but I've already been over everything with the police several times. I thought the man who did this was already on trial. Did I miss something?"

Noah gave her a disarming smile. "You've been very helpful, Ms. Crawley, but we just want to review a few things." He crossed his legs. "We talked to Professor Keenan yesterday, and he mentioned that Maggie was having financial troubles. I was wondering if you could tell me more about those."

Joanna brushed a piece of dark brown hair

from her face and pushed it behind her ear. "Sure, but I'm not sure why that matters now. I mean, Maggie was killed by a mugger in the park. Right? It didn't have anything to do with her work at the university."

"Everything matters," Sophia urged, leaning forward. "Even the smallest detail. Anything you can tell us about Maggie and the weeks before her death might be useful to us."

Joanna frowned, clearly unsure, but continued anyway. "Well, okay. It's not like I'm telling state secrets here." She bit her bottom lip. "About a week before Maggie died, her professor told her he wasn't going to renew her assistantship in the chemistry department. Maggie went ballistic. I mean, Keenan was her adviser, and he was basically holding her back so she wouldn't get her doctorate from Atlanta State for another year at least. Maybe longer. Maggie already had a boatload of student loans. She spent most of her days and evenings in the ASU chemistry lab or in that little room she called an office in the basement. Have you seen it?"

Sophia and Noah exchanged looks. "Yes, we've seen it," Noah confirmed. "But if their relationship was that bad, couldn't she just switch advisers?"

"If she switched advisers, she would have had to move to another discipline outside of the chemistry department." Joanna's eyes narrowed. "From what she said, Keenan would have prevented her from working with any of the other chemistry professors at Atlanta State. He's a pretty influential guy. Apparently, it's either his way or the highway. And going to another school wasn't an option. Maggie would have needed Keenan's recommendation to move, and they'd had some sort of disagreement, so I doubt Keenan would have given her a very good one. She also would have had to repeat a lot of the coursework that she had already completed."

Joanna shifted uncomfortably and motioned around her apartment. "This place is cheap, but without the assistantship, I don't think she could have afforded to stay here. Like I said, she was already struggling, and I don't think she could have gotten another job on the side. Keenan kept her pretty busy."

Sophia put up her hands. "So do you have any idea what happened between her and Keenan?"

Joanna shrugged and let her shoulders droop. "She never told me the details, and I am working on my master's in education.

It's a totally different department, so I'm not privy to the inner workings of the chemistry department—not that I would want to be. I know Professor Keenan drove her crazy, but she enjoyed the work and laughed off his criticisms, at least up until right before she died. She was furious with him then, but she never explained why she felt that way. I just figured they'd had some major disagreement about one of their projects."

Noah uncrossed his legs. "Is her stuff still in her room?"

Joanna shook her head. "No, sorry. I boxed it all up and put it in storage in the basement. I didn't know where to send it, and I needed to share expenses, so I have a new roommate living in Maggie's old room. She's not here right now or I'd introduce you."

Sophia took a few more notes, then looked back up and stowed her phone. "That's fine, but I would like to see what's in those boxes. Can you show us?"

Joanna stood. "Sure. I'll take you down there right now."

Sophia rose, a myriad of thoughts bouncing around in her head as she considered everything they had just learned. She was anxious to search through the containers and hoped they would find something, anything, that would help her finish this investigation, prove Prensky was innocent and bring Kylie safely back home. Time was running out, and her sister's life seemed to be slipping right through her fingers.

Sophia and Noah followed Joanna down her apartment stairs. Sophia wasn't anxious to go into another basement quite so soon, but she quelled the fear and pushed it down deep within her. Focus. She had to focus on saving Kylie. That was all that mattered.

She glanced over at Noah, who remained quiet throughout the questioning and was letting her take the lead. She knew they hadn't discovered much that was different from his original investigation, and so far, the new things they had learned hadn't pointed to a different perpetrator. Nonetheless, she had to keep searching, no matter what. She pushed away the discouragement that seemed to be choking her and resolved to just be as thorough as humanly possible. Hopefully, even if they didn't prove that Arlo was innocent, the kidnapper would realize that she had made a good-faith effort to comply with his demands and would release her sister unharmed, even if the jury came back with a guilty verdict.

Joanna led them to a small area in the basement that was divided into sections by chain-link fencing. Each section had a number on the gate that presumably corresponded to the apartment number of the owner. Joanna and Maggie's section held a few boxes and little else besides a bicycle, helmet and some Christmas decorations. Joanna pointed to a trunk and two small boxes in the back. "Those are hers. I donated her linens and clothing to charity, but what's left of her personal items is in those boxes." She opened the lock and hung it on a part of the fence. "Help yourself."

Noah pulled out his phone. "One more question. Do you recognize this man?" He showed her the picture of the hooded man who had tried to run them off the road.

Joanna glanced at the picture, then did a double take before forcing her features to take on a more neutral response. "He may be familiar…" she hedged.

Sophia took a step forward. "Please, tell us the truth. I can tell you recognize him. Like I said before, every little detail matters."

Joanna seemed to consider her words, then

finally shrugged. "Okay. I guess it doesn't matter much now anyway. That's Mark Ellis. He and Maggie were dating, but no one was supposed to know. I think they might have even gotten engaged before she died, but Maggie played the whole thing close to the vest."

Once again, Noah looked surprised. "Engaged? According to Professor Keenan, Maggie didn't have time to date anyone. Her entire life was supposed to revolve around chemistry. Are you sure?"

Joanna picked at her nails, obviously uncomfortable. "As sure as I can be. Look, Maggie and I were roommates, but we weren't best friends, and we didn't share a lot of confidences. To be honest, I didn't see her all that much. She slept here a lot, but our paths didn't cross very often. She would usually come home late, after I was already in bed, and I would leave early, when she was still sleeping. Our schedules didn't mesh."

While Joanna was speaking to Noah, Sophia pulled the top off the first box and started looking through the contents. There were a few books, some office supplies and photos. In the bottom, there was a thick folder with several paper-clipped papers inside. Sophia pulled out the folder and started sorting through it. Near the top, she discovered a printed draft of an article, along with a letter from the publisher, tentatively accepting the piece for publication in a national chemistry journal.

Sophia's brow furrowed. "Here's an article that has Maggie's name on it, and it looks like it was about to be published in a peer-reviewed journal. Do you know anything about it?"

Joanna took a step forward and took a look at what Sophia was showing her. "Sure. She was really excited about that about a month or so before she died, but then she quit mentioning it. I just figured something had happened and it didn't work out. Whenever she was home, she seemed to be working on it. She said it was her 'magnum opus.' You know, her 'great work.'"

"Do you know if it was ever published?"

"I have no idea. Chemistry isn't really my thing. She asked me to read it once, but I can't even understand what she's talking about in there."

Sophia flipped to another page. She didn't understand much of what she was reading, either, but it must have been important work if a national journal had considered publishing the document. "Do you think it's okay if I keep this copy? It might be relevant to our investigation."

Joanna nodded, then motioned to the lock. "Sure. Take what you want. Those boxes have been here for a while, and nobody has claimed them." She motioned to the apartment upstairs. "Is it okay if I leave you here and let you lock up on your way out? I've got a full schedule today, and I need to get back up to my apartment, grab a few things and head to the gym."

"Sure. We'll take care of it," Noah replied. "Thanks again for your time." He walked Joanna to the basement door and then returned to Sophia and started sorting through Maggie's things in the second box. "Find anything else interesting?"

Sophia closed the cover of the notebook she had been looking at and put it back in the trunk. She brushed some hair out of her eyes. "Nothing of interest." There had been some family photos, a few books and some cheap jewelry, but nothing she recognized as significant. She sighed and her shoulders slumped. "I feel like I'm looking for a needle in a haystack, with a timer ticking over my head, counting down the seconds."

Noah raised an eyebrow. "Do you think that paper you found means anything?"

"I don't know yet. If Arlo killed her as a random act of violence, then I doubt it matters. It's just too soon to tell. I do find it interesting that Professor Keenan complained about the quality of her work while, at the same time, a national chemistry publication was interested in her paper. I also find it interesting that Maggie was engaged and that her fiancé tried to kill us. I'm still not sure how this all fits together, though." She closed the lid on the trunk and replaced the boxes to their original location. "Ready to go?"

Noah followed her out of the storage area and locked the gate behind them. "Sure. I think our next stop should be to see Angie Carmichael."

"Who is she?"

Noah followed her up the stairs and out of the basement as he answered. "She's one of the other chemistry graduate students at Atlanta State University. She didn't have much to offer before, but I'm hoping she can shed some light on the importance of the paper you just found. This is the first I've heard of it."

"Do you really think it might be important?" Sophia asked as they made it outside of the building.

Noah grimaced. "I don't know. Like you said, it doesn't seem to have anything to do with Prensky or his actions. But something is definitely going on here. Why is this the first I've heard of it? It's like Keenan deliberately omitted it from our initial interviews. We need to know more."

"So why are we going to see Angie and not one of the other chemistry grad students?"

"She's the only one who seemed to know anything about Maggie," Noah answered. "The others knew her superficially, but Angie and Maggie both worked with Professor Keenan and occasionally worked on the same projects. After Maggie died, Angie got her research assistantship. I wouldn't say they were best friends, but at least they knew each other. Maybe Angie can give us some insight into the chemistry department at ASU."

"What about Maggie's fiancé?"

Noah met her eye. "What about him?"

Sophia stopped by the car door and waited while Noah unlocked it using the key fob in his hand. Then he surprised her by opening the door for her and motioning for her to get in. He closed the door after her and then circled the car, apparently keeping an eye out for danger. She appreciated his vigilance, but she couldn't keep the fear from sweeping over her.

She wasn't used to having her life in danger, and she had to admit the recent attempts to kill them both had unnerved her. As if she needed more stress in her life! At least she didn't have to go through all of this alone. Noah was being a good friend, and she was glad he was with her.

Once he was sitting in the driver's seat, she continued the conversation as he put the key in the ignition. "Well, if anyone knew Maggie, it would be the fiancé. Maybe he can offer us some insight into her life."

Noah started the car and navigated to the exit of the parking lot. "If we can get him to talk. Frankly, I'm more interested in knowing why he tried to kill us today."

Sophia laughed, but there was no mirth in her voice. "Yeah, me, too. I wonder…" Before she could even finish her sentence, a loud explosion sounded behind them.

NINE

Noah immediately slammed on the brakes, and Sophia huddled down against the seat. Seconds later, Noah covered her body with his own, protectively shielding her in case more devastation followed. A moment passed. Then another. When nothing else happened, the two of them slowly straightened and turned to see what had occurred behind them.

Maggie and Joanna's section of the apartment building no longer existed. Instead, smoke billowed around the rubble and pieces of soot and debris fell from the sky, littering the ground in all directions. Flames licked the wooden framing that remained, what little there was of it, and an acrid smell of burning plastic and other materials penetrated their nostrils, despite the fact that the car windows were tightly closed.

Sophia turned to Noah, her eyes wide.

She could sense the fear radiating from deep within her and felt helpless to stop it. Her entire body was trembling. When she spoke, her voice was breathless, as if she'd just run a mile. "Do you think…?"

"Yes, I think Joanna was in the apartment when it blew."

Tears swelled and rolled down Sophia's cheeks. "Oh, no. That poor woman. And who knows how many others were in that apartment building."

Noah quickly pulled out his phone and called in the blast with one hand, squeezing Sophia's hand with the other. She allowed the contact, aware that he was trying to offer her at least a small margin of comfort.

When he was done with the call, he stowed his phone again and turned back to Sophia. "Are you okay?" When she nodded, he continued. "I have to check for survivors and work the scene. I don't want to leave you here, but I really need to do my job. Can you stay here in the car, close by, so I can see you? I won't be able to do what I have to do if I'm worried about you and your safety at the same time that I'm trying to help others."

"I get it. I'll stay. Unless you think I can help?"

Noah shook his head vehemently. "No. For one thing, bomb sites are notoriously unstable. You could get hurt." He took her other hand and pressed them both between his. "We were also in that apartment only a few minutes ago. I think the killer just got unlucky. I imagine he was trying to kill us, too, but we left the premises just in the nick of time."

Another wave of fear swept over her. "That means you'll be a target out there—"

"I'll be careful," he said fervently. "But this is my job. I might be able to help someone. Please stay in the car." He met her eyes. "Please. I know I'm asking a lot, but I really need to know you're safe."

She wanted to argue, but she finally nodded and pulled her hands from his, while her respect for him grew exponentially. Despite the danger to himself, Noah was committed to helping people, and he was ready to go out there in the open if it meant he could save a life. He could have let others take the lead, but that just wasn't in his nature. He had to help. It was an impressive quality. One that she had rarely seen during her life. Such selflessness was inspiring.

He drove the car back to the demolished building and parked close enough that he could see Sophia sitting inside while he surveyed the damage and looked for survivors. She could already hear sirens approaching as first responders rushed to the scene.

Sophia stretched so she could keep an eye on him as he worked. The middle of the building had sunk into the ground below and now filled the space where the basement had been. From what she could tell, the blast had completely destroyed at least four apartments in that section of the building and damaged several others. Small, personal items were mixed with building debris. A flat-screen TV was now a ball of melted plastic and half of a refrigerator was recognizable beneath a pile of rubble. Dust still filled the air, and Sophia watched Noah pull out a handkerchief and tie it across his face to help filter the air so he could breathe. He also took off his tie and jacket and tossed them aside so he would have more freedom of movement.

Sophia lost sight of Noah for a moment and could suddenly hear sounds of the rubble settling. It was all she could do to stay in the car. A giant part of her wanted to leap out and verify that Noah was safe, but she fulfilled her promise and stayed in the vehicle, her face pressed against the glass. After several seconds, she saw him on the western side of the bomb site, yelling into the rubble, and relief swamped her. He looked up at one point and waved to her, letting her know he was okay, then continued working.

He picked his way around the edge of the scene, and Sophia said a heartfelt prayer, asking God to lead him to any survivors in time to save them.

Within minutes, the scene was full of emergency vehicles—fire, EMTs and police—their flashing lights filling the parking lot and bouncing off the remaining buildings. They quickly cordoned off the area to keep the onlookers back and out of the way.

She watched as Noah and some of the firefighters worked as a team to pull one middle-aged man from beneath a section of concrete. He appeared to have a broken arm and was scraped up, but he seemed otherwise unharmed. They were also able to save the man's dog, a big yellow Labrador. Unfortunately, they were not able to save Joanna Crawley. Sophia watched helplessly as her lifeless body was pulled from the debris, along with the body of another person who also hadn't survived. A third victim was later discovered. She didn't know the others and barely knew Joanna, but still her heart ached. These people had died because of her investigation. Guilt made her entire chest hurt.

Every few minutes, Noah glanced back over at his car, making sure that Sophia was still inside and no one dangerous had approached the vehicle.

The deeper they dug into this case, the more worried he became. This bombing had been way too close. If they had only lingered a few more minutes in the basement, or even in Maggie's apartment, they would probably be dead right now. A part of him wanted to take Sophia somewhere safe and hide her away from this horrible threat, but he just couldn't do it. He knew without a doubt that they had to continue the investigation—not only to save Sophia's sister but also to discover who was trying to stop them from re-investigating the case in the first place. The perpetrator had to be held accountable for this horrible and unnecessary loss of life.

Was Arlo Prensky innocent? Had he arrested the wrong man? A friend or relative of Prensky's certainly thought so, and was so convinced of his innocence that they were willing to kidnap a young girl to make the police take another look. On top of that, someone with a different agenda was willing to kill to make sure the case wasn't reopened. There was obviously more going on here than a simple crime of opportunity.

A painful knot formed in his stomach, twisting and turning. What had he missed? He didn't want to admit that he'd missed anything, but he had to face the facts.

He had to have missed something big.

A few hours later, he was released from the scene and had driven Sophia back to the police station. They'd stopped by a fast-food restaurant on the way. She hadn't wanted to order anything, but he had finally cajoled her into accepting a bag of fries and a small box of chicken nuggets. Then he ordered her favorite milkshake and even had them add whipped cream and a cherry to her shake to entice her to drink it.

He took another bite of his sandwich and leaned back in the conference room chair. He hadn't realized how hungry he was until he'd actually started to devour his food. To ensure the witness's safety, and their own, he and Sophia had asked their next interviewee to come to the station. That way, they would be surrounded by law enforcement officers, in case there was another threat, and they could at least try to ensure the interviewee's safety, as well.

Three murder attempts in two days was a new record for Noah, and he didn't want to go for four. The two of them had settled in the conference room, and Angie Carmichael, the other ASU grad student from the chemistry department, was due in about half an hour.

"Are you sure that's a good idea?" Noah asked. His eyebrow quirked as he watched Sophia dip her French fry in barbecue sauce. He couldn't imagine why anyone would want to do that, but she seemed quite happy with the arrangement.

At least she was eating. She had consumed precious little since this investigation had begun, even with his efforts this morning of fixing her a healthy breakfast. They had both skipped lunch and hadn't even stopped for a snack during the day. As a detective, he'd worked several high-pressure cases, and he had learned from personal experience how important it was to take care of himself during stressful situations. Sophia had seemed somewhat reserved since the bombing, so he hoped his joke about the fries would earn him a smile.

To his delight, she grinned and took another bite, making a humorous show of her actions. "I'm positive. I'm a Southern girl, through and through. This is how we do things here in the South." She dipped another fry and smacked her lips comically. "Yum!"

Noah shook his head, pleased that he had gotten what he was looking for and more. He found himself smiling, too, and realized that he had needed a stress-free moment, as well. She offered him a fry covered in barbecue sauce, but he shook his head and waved it away. "No, thank you. For the record, I consider myself a Southern guy, and that still doesn't look too appealing to me." He leaned forward and brushed a dab of sauce off her cheek. "Still, it's good to see you smile."

A moment passed and Sophia wiped her hands with a napkin. "There hasn't been much to smile about during the last couple of days," she said quietly, her smile fading.

Noah wanted that smile back. He gave her a playful nudge, despite the dust and bits of debris that still covered his clothing from his work at the bomb site. He hadn't wanted to take the time to change; it was more important to stay with Sophia. She didn't appear to mind the dirt, but she still wasn't herself. He tried again. "I seem to remember someone dipping Canadian bacon pizza into a little cup of ranch dressing back in high school."

She laughed again, but it wasn't as full, and a sadness filled her countenance. He couldn't blame her. The stress of having her life threatened over and over again and her sister being kidnapped had to be weighing heavily on her. Still, she had a wistful look in her eyes as she thought of the pleasant memory they had shared. She met his eyes. "You actually remember that? I haven't had Canadian bacon pizza in a long time. I'm not sure it's even available anymore."

Noah leaned back in his chair, suddenly somber himself. He'd been waiting for a chance to talk to her about their past, but there never seemed to be an opportunity. Maybe now was as good a time as ever. Perhaps he could at least clear the air between them.

He ran his hand through his hair as nervousness suddenly swept through him. Where should he start? He sighed and pressed on. "I remember a lot of things. I remember playing some awful tricks on my very dear friend and pushing her away. I'm really sorry, Sophia. I know this probably isn't the best time and place to talk about this, but I was horrible to you. I want you to know how much I regret how I treated you back then."

Sophia pushed away her milkshake. The topic had obviously been weighing on her, too.

Maybe it had been the right time to bring it up.

"Why *did* you do those things? I never understood what I had done to hurt you so badly that you felt like humiliating me was the answer."

The knot in his stomach intensified as he watched her aimlessly push around the barbecue sauce packets on the table. Maybe he should have at least waited until she'd eaten more of her dinner before bringing up such a delicate subject. He grimaced, struggling for the right words. Like a Band-Aid coming off a wound, maybe it was better to just say it quickly and hope for the best.

He looked away, unable to meet her eyes. "I was in love with you. When you didn't return my feelings, my pride got in the way. I was hurt and angry that you didn't love me back."

She was silent for a full minute, and he sat there, holding his breath, waiting for her to speak. Every muscle in his body felt as tightly wound as a guitar string.

Finally, she raised her eyebrow. "So, you thought that if you hurt me badly enough, I'd change my mind and fall in love with you?"

He shrugged helplessly. "No, not really. I didn't think you'd ever change your mind. I guess the bottom line was that I wanted you to hurt like I was hurting. I know sometimes even the best of friends grow apart, but I didn't want to lose you. When you didn't share my feelings, I struck back and behaved badly. I wish I had a better reason, but I just don't. I was a real mess back then, and I was more focused on impressing my friends than thinking about your feelings." He shrugged helplessly again. "I was a dumb, immature kid. I was horrible to you, and I was very, very wrong. Please forgive me."

He turned to look at her and was once again taken aback by her beauty, both inside and out. He felt a heaviness in his chest as he waited for her to react and respond. Was he still holding his breath? He couldn't tell because he was concentrating so hard on trying to read her expression and her body language as he sat there, hoping for absolution.

She didn't speak, and he still had no idea

what she was thinking, no matter how much he studied her face. Could she tell that those old feelings of attraction were starting to re-surface in him? He wondered how much she had surmised as they'd worked this case to-gether. Part of him wanted to share his grow-ing feelings, but he was still afraid of her rejection. He leaned forward, and when she didn't pull away, he took both of her hands and held them gently. Electricity seemed to sizzle between them at his touch. He locked his eyes with hers. "Can we leave the past in the past? Please, Sophia. Please forgive me."

She finally gave him a nod, although her look was wistful, as if she was still consider-ing his words. "I do forgive you, Noah. And you should know, it wasn't all your fault. I could have been nicer back then—more un-derstanding." She swallowed but didn't pull her hands away. "I guess it was a difficult time for both of us. We should have talked when things first started to fall apart. I... I didn't realize how you felt."

He sighed in relief. "You're right. We should have talked." He pulled her hands up and brushed his lips over her knuckles. "Thank you for forgiving me." He tilted his head. "Do you think we can be friends again?"

She laughed, and Noah felt the ball of stress that had settled in his chest slowly start to dissipate. Her forgiveness made a strange feeling of contentment sweep over him from head to toe. It was a wonderful start to rebuilding the bond they had shared.

"Yes, I think we can be friends. Let's give this relationship a second chance, shall we?"

He smiled, released her hands and pushed her milkshake over in front of her again. "Okay, friend. Please eat. I'm worried about you. You haven't eaten hardly anything in the last two days."

She did as he asked and picked up the cup. He leaned back, relieved that they had finally talked and put the past to rest. It was as if a giant weight had finally been removed from his shoulders—a weight he hadn't even really understood that he was carrying. Why had he waited so long to seek forgiveness? He should have initiated contact years ago. He'd wasted entirely too much time nurturing the regret and embarrassment he'd felt as a result of his actions.

He watched Sophia take a sip of her milkshake and push some of her hair behind her ear in a motion that was familiar and feminine at the same time. A new wave of attraction swept over him, but he looked away, trying to hide his reaction. What would she think if she knew the old feelings of attraction were resurfacing? And it wasn't completely one-sided this time—at least, he didn't think so. Despite their situation, he could tell there was a mutual magnetism building between the two of them. He could feel it.

But would she ever love him?

Attraction wasn't love.

And was she really feeling anything right now for him besides gratitude?

He wasn't quite sure about how to move forward, so he closed his eyes and prayed for guidance and direction, right there in the conference room.

TEN

Sophia sipped her drink thoughtfully, a host of emotions running through her heart. She was happy they had finally discussed the past, but she still found his youthful profession of love disconcerting. Sure, Noah had tried to take her out on a date a few times, but she had never understood the depth of his feelings. He sure hadn't acted like he was in love. In fact, all of this time, she'd thought she had offended him and had somehow been to blame for their relationship's failure. It was a relief to understand what had really happened and why he had treated her so poorly.

But she still didn't trust him.

He was an excellent law enforcement officer. She had witnessed that firsthand. And he had gone above and beyond trying to help her save Kylie. She knew without a doubt that God had brought him back into her life for a reason, and she trusted him completely with her sister's fate.

But trusting him with her heart was an entirely different matter.

Yes, time had passed, and they had both grown and matured. They could be friends again, and maybe after this was all over, they would share a dinner or two and reminisce. She could tell there was an attraction brewing between them, but she didn't have to act on it. Noah Bradley was a good-looking man, with shoulders that made her knees go weak and eyes that could see into her soul. She even found herself tingling at his touch. But these new feelings didn't erase the old hurt, despite the forgiveness she had offered, and she wanted to make very sure that she wasn't confusing attraction for gratitude.

A knock on the conference room door broke into her concentration and she put down the remains of her French fries and took a sip from her shake.

"Detective? Ms. Archer? You've got a visitor."

Noah nodded and walked over to thank the deputy who had stuck his head in. Then he welcomed Angie Carmichael, who had been standing behind the officer, and invited her to take a seat at the large, rectangular conference table.

The woman was lithe and clothed professionally in a dark blue dress. The nautical-print silk scarf around her neck set off her hazel eyes, and she had an earnestness about her that made her seem approachable and friendly. Despite all appearances, she also looked haggard. There were tiny stress lines around her mouth and dark circles under her eyes. Creases were visible on her forehead and between her eyebrows. Sophia had made reading people into an art form, but this woman was sending so many contradictory signals it was hard to tell what to believe. Was she friendly and overworked or difficult and vindictive? Sophia pulled out her phone and got ready to take notes, curious about what the woman would add, if anything, to the investigation.

"Ms. Carmichael? I'm Sophia Archer. Thanks so much for joining us."

Angie put her purse down by her feet. "Sure. It's not a problem, but I'm not sure how I can help. Isn't the man who killed Maggie in jail?"

"He is," Noah agreed as he took his seat.

"But we've had some new evidence come up, and we wanted your insight."

Sophia pushed aside the remnants of her meal and thumbed through her notes. "Can you tell me about Professor Keenan?"

Angie looked a bit taken aback, suddenly nervous. "What about him?"

Sophia glanced at Noah, wondering if he was seeing the same body language that she was. Something wasn't right, although she couldn't put her finger on exactly what was going on. "We were hoping you could tell us what it's like to work with him. He is your faculty adviser for your doctorate in chemistry, correct?"

Angie smiled and visibly relaxed. "He is now. I started working with him after Maggie died. He's amazing and quite the scientist. I'm really learning a lot."

Sophia blinked. She hadn't expected the exuberant response, especially since the man had left such a negative impression in her mind. "We understand Maggie's assistantship was going to be canceled in the fall. Do you know anything about that?"

"I do. In the spring, Professor Keenan told me she was doing substandard work and the position might be available if I worked really hard and showed him my potential. He offered me the position shortly after Maggie died. He said he didn't want to be disrespectful, but he had some projects in the works that just couldn't wait, so he needed me to start immediately."

She leaned forward, as if telling a secret. "Professor Keenan is incredibly intelligent and was recently published in a major national journal. He wrote an article that was cutting-edge. It's bringing all sorts of notoriety to the university. It's really an honor to be able to work with him. He's well-known, both nationally and internationally, in the scientific field. I'm sure that once I earn my doctorate, I'll be able to just mention he was my adviser and write my own ticket wherever I want to go."

Sophia tilted her head. She wasn't so sure Ms. Carmichael's assessment was correct, but it wasn't worth arguing about. "Tell us more about this article."

Angie smiled. "It's about the reasons for instability in an inorganic compound named perovskite. Unless you have a background in chemistry, it's hard to understand."

Noah and Sophia glanced at one another again, and Angie took that as an invitation to continue. "You see, the source of the thermodynamic instability in perovskite is the inorganic cesium atom. The atom actually 'rattles' within the crystal structure, causing the entire compound to be instable."

Sophia glanced up at Noah, who also was clearly lost by Angie's explanation. The chemistry student was pleased at their reaction, and a haughty smirk spread across her face as she realized they hadn't followed her description. Sophia could suddenly tell that the woman's initial friendly appearance had all been an act. She was now aggressive in both her stance and tone. Finally, the chemistry student's true personality had surfaced.

Sophia wondered why the woman was so disingenuous and how her behavior related to Maggie's death, if at all. There were a lot of difficult people in the world, but just because Angie bore several unlikable personality traits, it didn't mean she was guilty of murder—or of any other crime. "Okay, then," she said quickly, ready to move on to a different topic. "Did you use one of the desks downstairs in the basement office suite where Maggie was working?"

"I did, but a couple of weeks ago, I was

moved to a new office on the third floor so I could be closer to Professor Keenan's office."

That was an interesting tidbit. Sophia pushed forward. "Did you know that someone had installed a cell phone blocker in that office?"

"Sure," Angie said as she crossed her legs. "Some of the other grad students had a problem with talking on the phone when they were supposed to be working. They were constantly taking personal calls. It was very frustrating, so I asked Professor Keenan to put a blocker in there so I wouldn't be so distracted."

"So, he's the one who installed it?" Noah asked.

"Yes. He did it for me. He said he didn't want anything to come between me and my studies."

"Did you know that cell phone jammers are illegal?" Noah asked.

Angie frowned. "I don't know why they should be. It made it much easier to get my job done. You must be mistaken. Maggie and those other students are the ones who were breaking the rules. They knew they weren't supposed to constantly be on their phones, but they thought they could get away with whatever they wanted if they were down in the basement."

"Was Maggie one of the students constantly using her phone?" Sophia asked quietly, ignoring the woman's previous comments.

"She was," Angie agreed. "I think she had a boyfriend, but I could never prove it."

"Why would you want to prove it, and to whom?" Noah asked.

Angie gave Noah a frown. "Why, to Professor Keenan, of course. And the reason is simple. Professor Keenan demands that we stay focused on our main objective—completing our chemistry projects. Other relationships get in the way. Maggie should have known that. She was Professor Keenan's research assistant at the time. The rules had been explained to her in some detail, yet she was constantly breaking them."

Sophia grimaced, unable to continue keeping her opinions to herself. This woman was really a piece of work. "Have you ever heard of a work-life balance?"

Angie sat straighter in her chair. "Not in grad school and not in Professor Keenan's chemistry department."

Sophia was tempted to argue, but decided it would be a waste of breath. Although clearly intelligent, Angie also seemed to have very definite ideas about certain things, and she probably wasn't going to change her mind in the next ten minutes.

Sophia moved on. "Did you see Maggie the day she died?"

Angie nodded. "Yes. She went down to the basement office, changed in one of the bathrooms and then said she was going on a walk in the park. That's the last time I saw her."

"Are you having a romantic relationship with Professor Keenan?" Noah asked out of the blue.

Sophia's and Angie's heads both snapped to look at Noah, but his face was blank of emotion as he waited for a response.

"I don't see how that's any of your business," Angie finally sputtered.

"It matters if Professor Keenan killed Maggie so he could replace her with you," Noah responded, his tone even.

"He didn't!" Angie said hotly as she pushed away from the table and stood. "He would never hurt anyone. Professor Keenan is an amazing mentor, but Maggie never appreciated him or his skills. Then she got involved with someone, and her work began to suffer. I can't help it if she was going to lose her job. I am not responsible for her behavior. I *earned* that assistantship." She glared at the two of them and then leaned down to pick up her purse. "I have nothing more to say to either of you. Good day." She turned and left the room, slamming the door behind her.

Sophia put her phone on the table and whistled. "Wow. She is really something."

Noah shook his head. "She was nothing like that when I interviewed her before. Back then, she was all tears, and kept expressing her undying friendship and loyalty to Maggie, who had been taken too soon. Good grief! She's a consummate actress!"

"I was thinking the same thing." Sophia pulled out a notebook from her bag and put the paper she had discovered at Maggie's apartment in front of Noah. "Do you see the title of this article?"

Noah picked it up and read the title out loud. "'Perovskite Instability.'"

Sophia met his eye. "Is it me, or did Angie just tell us that Professor Keenan had a motive for murder?"

ELEVEN

"What do you mean?" Noah asked. "You think Professor Keenan murdered Maggie to get her out of the way so he could have a relationship with Angie?"

Sophia shook her head, and her brown eyes flashed. Even her cheeks were flushed. Noah thought she had never looked more magnificent, despite the circumstances. Sophia was in her element. It was no wonder she was such a successful investigative reporter. No matter what, she kept digging until she discovered the truth, and she was passionate about her work. Her zeal was obvious based on the drive and determination she had exhibited just over the past couple of days.

"No, I don't think he was after Angie initially, although I think you hit the nail on the head when you asked her about their current relationship. It's pretty obvious something is going on there now, even if it wasn't before. If my suspicions are correct, however, I think there's even more going on here beyond a physical relationship. Let me make some calls, and then I'll know if my suspicions are correct."

"Okay," Noah said thoughtfully. "I want to check on Maggie's fiancé anyway and ask him why he tried to kill us today. Last I heard, he was in the building and still being processed, but I'm sure they're done by now. He's probably waiting down in Interrogation. Can you make your calls from here while I go ask him some questions?"

Sophia smiled. "Unless your boss installed a cell phone blocker while we were out."

Noah laughed. "Okay. I'll be back in a few. Make yourself at home."

Detective Matthews met Noah by his desk before he even made it down to the interrogation room. "Hey, Detective. Where's Ms. Archer?"

"In the conference room making some calls."

Matthews put his hand on his chin, as if making an appraisal, and studied Noah from head to toe. "You've looked better, my friend."

Noah glanced at his clothing and sighed. He had to admit, his colleague was right. He'd forgotten to retrieve his tie and jacket at the bomb site, and his pants, shirt and shoes were definitely ruined beyond repair. His hair was dusty and filled with particles of wood and concrete debris. Even his hands were dirty and scraped, and he needed some basic first aid.

Matthews was the fashion statement of the office, second only to Roman, and he always seemed to look impeccable. At times, Noah admired the detectives' polished and professional appearances, but now wasn't one of them. "Yeah, I know, but I can't worry about my appearance right now, Matthews. A girl's life is at stake. In fact, I haven't even been able to think straight since Sophia walked into our office. This case is extremely time sensitive."

Matthews nodded knowingly. "Ah, so it's a lack of time that's the reason you're discombobulated, is that it?"

Noah narrowed his eyes, not missing the gibe. He knew others had noted his commitment to this case and his attraction to Sophia, but he wasn't ready to be teased about it. They were a close unit of very adept investigators. Little passed by without notice. "If you have something helpful to say, then say it. Otherwise…"

The detective raised his hands in mock surrender. "Okay, okay, Mr. Sensitive. You act like someone's tried to kill you twice today."

That made Noah smile. It wasn't Matthews's fault they weren't making much progress. Normally, Noah could take a ribbing without a second thought. He shook his head. "Sorry. I guess I'm just tired."

His colleague said nothing more about it, but his eyes said he saw the truth. Still, the man was gracious enough to change the subject, and Noah was grateful. "Where are you headed?" Matthews asked.

"I was going down to talk to Maggie's fiancé, who tried to run us off the road today. I'm hoping he can explain why he tried to kill us."

Matthews shook his head. "Don't waste your time. He's still being processed. They're backed up down there, and he had to be taken to the ER first anyway for a medical exam. I'd give them another thirty minutes or so."

Noah squeezed the back of his office chair, frustrated. "Has he said anything at all?"

The detective shook his head. "Not yet. Nobody's really taken a good run at him, though. Do you want us to hold off until you can join in?"

"Yeah, come get me when he's ready, okay?"

Matthews nodded and started to turn, but Noah still had questions. "Wait. Before you go... Has anything new broken in this case?"

"Not that I know of. Charlie asked me to do background research on some of Prensky's more suspicious-looking relatives. So far, I haven't found anything new. I've interviewed a few of them, but they've all had verifiable alibis and haven't been near Flint Rock."

"What about his uncle, John Prensky?"

Matthews shifted. "He was the first one I checked. His alibi was solid."

"Okay. Thanks, Matthews. Like I said before, I owe you one." He returned to the conference room, where Sophia was just finishing up a call. He could tell by her body language that she had discovered something new. She was sitting taller and her face was animated and full of vigor.

She motioned for him to sit, said a few final words on the phone, then hung up and faced him. "Well, I just uncovered some very interesting news."

"Such as?"

"Well, it looks like Maggie had not only been working on her dissertation with Professor Keenan—she had also done the bulk of the man's research and writing on the article he published under his name alone. In fact, she was the primary author. I called the editor and discussed it with him. I mentioned the copy we found in Maggie's basement. It turns out that version was one of the last drafts of the article, and it only had Maggie's name on it. According to the editor, Maggie spoke in detail about the work and was able to answer several questions he had about the methodology and the conclusions."

She paused and took a breath. "In other words, it was clear that she was the author, not Keenan. However, a couple of weeks later, the editor received a newer version with some minor changes, and Maggie's name had been replaced with Keenan's. When the editor asked about it, Keenan told him that he'd asked Maggie to handle the submission process because he was just too busy to deal with it, but that he had always planned to step in once the article was accepted and ready for publication. He claimed he had always been the primary author."

Noah shook his head. "Wow."

"Wow is right," Sophia agreed.

"And the editor believed Keenan?" Noah asked, pursing his lips.

Sophia nodded, her eyes bright. "Sure. He's a tenured professor at a major university. Apparently, Maggie called the editor the week before she died and complained when she found out what Keenan had done, but he told her she had to work it out with Keenan, or they would just cancel the article's publication altogether. Then Keenan called the man after Maggie's death. He claimed that he and Maggie had worked out their differences and the article should be published in his name alone."

Noah leaned back, amazed. "Unbelievable."

Sophia grimaced. "Yes, that man is not only remarkably offensive—he's apparently a thief, as well. Anyway, I then called the chair over at ASU who heads up the science department. It turns out that Professor Keenan was under pressure to publish and his job was in peril." She leaned back herself and bit her bottom lip. "What do you think?"

"I'd say he definitely had motive," Noah conceded. "And I think you've done a great job. But you have to understand, having a motive doesn't make him guilty. Even if Keenan stole the article and got it published in his name, that makes him despicable. It doesn't make him a murderer."

"Well, what about his relationship with Angie?"

Noah shrugged. "Again, he's contemptible, and he had a motive, but that doesn't make him a killer."

Sophia nudged her phone a few inches back and forth as she considered his words, obviously frustrated. She finally pushed her chair back from the table, stood and started pacing. "You're right. And I know you're right." She tucked a strand of her hair behind her ear. "I was ready to march over to the university and arrest Keenan, but having motive isn't enough. We need proof he actually committed the murder." She turned to face him. "I'm sorry." She rubbed her forehead. "I guess I'm just desperate to get Kylie back, so I'm grasping at straws."

Noah stood, approached her and reached over to take her hand. "Hey, you've done an amazing job," he said gently. "A lot of what you've discovered is new evidence that we never uncovered during the original investigation. There's just one important fact that we can't overlook—Arlo Prensky's DNA was found at the crime scene. If Keenan is the murderer, how did Prensky's DNA get there?"

Sophia gritted her teeth and drew her lips into a thin line as frustration and stress overwhelmed her. She felt tears threatening, but she didn't want to release them. She didn't mind crying in front of Noah, but she was afraid that if she allowed herself to cry, she wouldn't be able to stop. "I'm so scared, Noah. What if they kill her? What if she's already dead?"

"We can't give up hope," Noah said vehemently. "We'll keep looking until we find her."

Sophia was about to respond when her phone beeped with a notification. She dropped Noah's hand and went back over to the conference table. Picking up her phone, she swiped to the correct screen. When she saw what had arrived, she turned quickly and held up the phone to show him. "It's a video of Kylie! Look!"

Noah moved quickly to her side and bent his head so he could see her screen and they could watch together. Kylie was again secured with zip ties like in the first photo the kidnapper had provided, and she was sitting in a chair surrounded by boxes. Faint red marks could be seen around her wrists and ankles. Her eyes were puffy as if she'd been crying, and also had dark circles under them. Sophia hit the play button and her heart clenched as the video commenced.

"Sophie! Please help me! I'm so scared. They said they're going to kill me if you don't do what they ask. Whatever they want, please give it to them. I want to come home! Please, Sophia, help me."

The video ended, and Sophia started shaking so badly she had to put the phone on the table so she wouldn't drop it. She covered her mouth with her hand, trying to bring herself under control before she spoke.

Noah put his hand on Sophia's shoulder and squeezed it gently. "Okay," he said forcefully, "let's get this phone to Roman. Come with me."

They found Roman at his desk in the middle of researching some of the information found in the box of newspaper clippings. He was typing furiously on the keyboard and staring intensely at the screen.

"Making any progress?" Noah asked.

"Not so far," Roman answered, his voice baring his frustration as he turned from his keyboard. "What have you got?"

Sophia showed him the video on her cell and he quickly took the phone and forwarded a copy of the video to his computer. He then downloaded the video onto a small flash drive and handed it to her. "Here. You can analyze this in the conference room while I see if I can track down the source from your phone. Let me keep your cell for a minute or two. I'll bring it back to you shortly."

Sophia handed the USB to Noah and he grabbed a laptop from his desk as they made their way back to the conference room. En route, Noah pulled in Detective Matthews, who immediately set aside the file he had been reading and jumped up to join them. She was glad Noah was getting help. Fresh eyes never hurt, and she could tell Noah was tiring, despite the new adrenaline the video had obviously pumped through his veins. She realized, like he did, that this short clip was probably the best clue they had right now.

Once in the conference room, the three of them sat at the large table. Noah opened his laptop, connected it wirelessly to a large wall-mounted screen and brought up the video so they could all see it.

"Sophia, we're going to have to watch this again—a few times, actually. We want to look for anything that will give us a clue as to Kylie's whereabouts. It's going to be difficult for you to see. Would you rather wait at my desk so you don't have to go through this?"

Sophia took a moment to think. True, it would be hard to see Kylie's pleas for help over and over again, but if it helped them find her, Sophia would walk on hot coals to save her sister.

"I want to stay. Maybe I'll see something important."

Noah nodded and started the video. They watched it twice before Noah stopped it on the last frame. "Okay, what do you all see?"

Sophia tilted her head slightly as she tried to focus on everything in the video other than the anguish in Kylie's voice. "She's wearing a T-shirt I bought her for Christmas. She looks tired, so I don't think she's had much sleep."

"Good." Noah nodded. "What else?"

"She was trembling," Sophia added. "But I think it was from cold, not just because she's scared. This time of year, she usually wears a hoodie or sweater almost every day, even if it's sunny outside."

"Okay, that's great information. That means she's probably somewhere that's not heated—or at least not heated well." Noah ran the video back again. "This time, listen to her words. Is there anything special about what she says or how she says it?"

They each listened carefully, but none of them heard anything out of the ordinary, even when the volume was turned up to maximum level.

"No sounds in the background. No motors running, no traffic, so they're probably not near a major highway," Matthews observed.

"Wait," Sophia said quickly. "I want to focus on the background noise again. Is there any way to lower the voice and bring up the background sounds?"

Noah nodded, fiddled with the controls and then played the video again. This time, they could faintly hear an electronic beeping.

"That sounds like some sort of machine that is backing up," Matthews opined.

Noah nodded, made another adjustment on the controls, then played it again. They heard the beeping and a small amount of engine noise. Both sounds were clearly coming from some sort of machinery that was reversing.

"Who needs heavy equipment that beeps like that—a construction site? Maybe a warehouse or storage facility?" Matthews asked.

"I don't think a construction trailer or a warehouse would necessarily have good heating, even in an office. If she's being held in a part of the warehouse that's open, it could still have very poor heating and cooling. Most of those types of buildings usually have high ceilings and little to no insulation," Noah noted.

The group was considering the possibilities when Roman knocked, entered and handed Sophia her cell phone. "I can't trace the video transmission. The signal bounced between too many IP addresses. I'm really sorry. Whoever we're dealing with has some decent computer skills."

"Thanks, Roman. Want to check this video out with us?" Noah asked. "An extra set of eyes can't hurt."

Roman agreed and took the chair next to Matthews as Noah cued up the video again after explaining what they'd already discovered. "Okay. This time, look at the surroundings. What can we see in the room where they are holding her?"

They watched the video twice more and then went back to watch it frame by frame.

"Stop. Okay, look. I see old seventies-style paneling in the background. You know—that wooden stuff in about six-inch vertical sections?" Roman stood, walked over to the screen and pointed to the paneling he had noted. "See? That means wherever they are holding her, it's an older building."

Noah stood, as well, and stepped closer to the screen. He pointed to a stack of boxes to Kylie's right, one of which had a sticker on the side. "Can anyone read this? It looks like it's referring to some sort of flower festival." He pointed to a design in the upper left corner of the sticker. "Isn't that a cherry?"

Roman moved over to the laptop and blew up the section of the video where the sticker was visible. The picture was highly pixelated, but they were still able to see it a bit better.

Noah pointed again. "I think that's a cherry and flowers, and I think that word is 'March.' So maybe this box is supposed to go to some festival or other event that has something to do with flowers or fruit?" He turned, his hands on his hips. "Maybe Kylie is being held in a warehouse that provides some sort of item to a March festival?"

Sophia's heart started beating even harder against her chest. It wasn't much, but it was a lead. Maybe, just maybe, they were one step closer to finding Kylie.

TWELVE

"So, you're Maggie Spencer's fiancé," Noah said caustically as he tossed a file on the table across from Mason Tucci, who was sitting in the interrogation room chair, handcuffed to a metal bar fastened to the tabletop. It was late, and he was tired, but Noah had to conduct this interview before the day was over. He knew that Kylie's time was running out, and he needed to do everything possible to find her before it was too late.

He glanced at the man who looked just about as beat up as Noah felt. His face was bruised, marked with angry red scratches, thanks to the airbag deployment. His hands were marred with scabs and cuts from the windshield glass. A couple of deeper wounds had been sewn closed on his face, the black synthetic stitching making his injuries appear even more severe than they actually were. At least his bloody clothes had been traded for a set of scrubs at the hospital.

"We interviewed Professor Keenan a few days ago. He says Maggie didn't have time for a relationship. He claims she was too busy."

"Keenan doesn't know spit," Tucci grumbled. "And, yes, I was Maggie's fiancé, until she was viciously murdered."

"And you thought killing Ms. Archer and me would bring her back?" Noah asked, unable to keep the anger from his voice.

"You were trying to get her killer off. You want that animal Prensky to go free."

Noah's brow furrowed. "What are you talking about?"

"Prensky killed my fiancée!" Tucci snarled, his tone derisive. "He deserves to go to prison for the rest of his life. You and that investigative reporter reopened the case. Now you're trying to prove that he's innocent. I want somebody to pay for Maggie's murder."

Noah rubbed his forehead. "You started following us from the courthouse. Don't you realize that the only reason I was at the courthouse in the first place was to testify *against* Prensky? I'm the one who arrested him!"

"Yeah, so you say. But like I said, that Archer woman you were with is an investigative reporter. She wants to get Prensky off."

Noah threw up his hands, knowing there were only a handful of people who knew the motivation behind Sophia's investigation. How could this man know anything about it at all? "What? Where did you get that idea?"

Tucci shrugged.

"Oh, no," Noah said, shaking his head. "That didn't just pop into your head. Who told you that?"

Tucci still didn't respond. Instead, he leaned back in his chair and slouched, as if totally disengaging from the entire conversation. The man's body language made Noah even angrier, but he realized that getting upset wasn't going to make the man talk. He tried a different tactic.

"We found out that Professor Keenan was trying to publish an article on perovskite. Do you know anything about that?"

This topic got Tucci's interest. He slowly straightened. But he fisted his hands and pulled against the cuffs so hard that red marks started to appear by his wrists. "The man is a thief. Maggie wrote that article."

Noah shrugged, intentionally goading Tucci, hoping he would talk and divulge something useful that would help their investigation. There was definitely more going on here than met the eye, but so far, the pieces just weren't fitting together in this puzzle. "I don't know. Ms. Archer talked to Professor Keenan. He claimed he wrote the article."

"He can claim it all day long. That doesn't make it true."

"I think the same can be said of your fiancée. Do you have any proof?"

Tucci hit the table with both hands. "He stole that article! Maggie did all the work, and then he deleted her name, put his name on it and took all the credit. I saw her do the work. I witnessed it with my own two eyes. He's the one who needs to go to prison. Not me."

Aha. Now they were getting somewhere. "Again, what proof do you have?"

Tucci's body deflated. "None. That's my problem. When Prensky killed her, he took her laptop and hard drive. Everything that proved it was on that computer. Maggie didn't believe in using cloud storage. She said it wasn't safe. And now somebody's blown up her apartment. If there was anything left, it's gone now."

"Ms. Archer found a copy of an earlier draft of the article with Maggie's name on it."

Tucci leaned forward. "Then you know I'm telling the truth!"

"Actually, I do know. But one prior draft is circumstantial. Anyone could have put her name on it and printed it. What we need is the laptop to pursue that scenario or a hard drive with the previous versions. Then we could see the properties of the various documents." Noah tapped the table with his fingers. "Do you think Keenan had anything to do with Maggie's death?"

Tucci narrowed his eyes. "I thought so at the beginning. But then you arrested Prensky. It has to be Prensky, right? Otherwise, you arrested the wrong guy."

Noah straightened, trying to show more confidence in his prior actions than he really felt. "I still think Prensky killed Maggie. We got the right man. His DNA was at the scene." He rubbed his chin. "But what I want to know is how you found out Ms. Archer was interested in the case in the first place. It's not like she took out a billboard. Why did you target her?"

Again, Tucci shut down and refused to answer, so Noah opened the file folder he had brought in and pushed it forward. "I checked you out, Mr. Tucci. I saw how you were a student at ASU in the computer science department until you dropped out in December, and I see how you have a job at Protel, the regional cell phone company. You've worked there almost two years."

"So?"

"So, here's what I think. I think you got suspicious of Professor Keenan when you discovered he put a cell phone blocker in Maggie's office. I think you knew he was taking advantage of Maggie and stole her work, and after he stole her paper, I think you cloned his cell phone so you could hear his conversations and get the proof you needed to show that he was a thief." Noah narrowed his eyes. "I think you're still listening, and I think you overheard our conversation with Keenan when Ms. Archer was asking him questions, and you didn't like her asking those questions. I think you decided to do something about it."

Tucci had the nerve to look surprised, but he was a very bad actor. It was obvious from the expression on his face that Noah had hit the nail on the head.

"I think I need an attorney."

"That's the smartest thing you've said all day." Noah closed the file and stood. "I'm sorry your fiancée was killed, Mr. Tucci. I really am. But that doesn't give you the right to hurt other people, especially innocent ones. Ms. Archer wants to verify the truth about what happened to Maggie—no more, no less. She wants to follow the evidence wherever it leads and make sure we got the right guy. And you almost killed her for that."

He walked to the door, satisfied that there was nothing more to get from this man. The anger he had felt toward Mason Tucci had dissipated, and now he just felt sorry for him. Maggie's fiancé was going to prison for attempted murder—all because he had misread a situation and acted with his emotions instead of his head. Now his entire life would be changed forever because of one very bad decision. Noah ran his fingers through his hair, then fisted his hands. Maybe he could learn something from this guy.

Sophia awoke with a start, her body cramped from the awkward position she had been sleeping in. She massaged her neck, trying to work out the kinks, and sat slowly, groggily remembering where she was and why she was there. Conference room. Atlanta Police Department. Kylie. She was still in her chair since she had fallen asleep on her laptop keyboard. She wondered how many of the keys were now indented on her cheek. She rubbed her face absently, hoping she hadn't drooled on the keyboard.

She stretched and glanced around the conference room. Someone had turned the overhead fixture off, but she could still see because of the ambient light coming from four laptops, the LCD screen, and the safety flashlights plugged in on two of the conference room walls.

She stood and ambled over to the inside window that let her see the detectives' bullpen. The light was low there, too, but she could make out a couple of figures. Roman was asleep at his desk, his arm thrown haphazardly across the back of his chair, pillowing his head. Noah was the only other person in the room. Still in the clothes he had been wearing during the bombing, he had pulled two of the office chairs together to create a makeshift bed.

She leaned against the window frame, still rubbing her cheek, and studied Noah. Normally clean-shaved, his beard now shadowed his face, giving him a mischievous appearance. His features showed his exhaustion, and she saw stress lines around his eyes, even in

sleep. Even so, he was incredibly handsome
and a whisper of attraction swept over her
from head to toe. Some might not have found
him as attractive as she did, but she loved his
rugged features, high cheekbones and broad
shoulders.

Sophia shifted but continued her perusal.
His face seemed almost boyish in the low
light, and she was reminded suddenly of a
time when they had been ten or so and they'd
gone wandering around on a friend's farm.
They came back as dirty as could be, yet
full of excitement. It had been a day filled
with adventure, and they had explored, play-
acted, danced and just enjoyed each other's
company for the entire day. Life had been so
simple then. Her biggest worries had been
how to get the ketchup stain off her shirt and
making sure she was home by six each night.
Noah had been her best friend, and even running around the neighborhood, they had spent
hours together on a regular basis. She missed
those days.

She stopped her woolgathering and glanced
at the clock mounted over the conference
room door. It was a little after 6:00 a.m. She
went in search of a bathroom and then quietly returned to the conference room. Still

alone, she glanced out the window again and noticed that Roman was no longer sleeping in his chair and had disappeared. Only Noah was still sleeping, but she didn't want to wake him. She stretched and yawned, but then sat again in front of her laptop. She'd only gotten a few hours of rest, but she didn't think she could sleep any longer, despite the fatigue that was making her mind feel fuzzy. A moment later, she noticed that someone had brought in a box of Danish pastries and put it on the table. There was a sticker on the top, letting everyone know that the filling was cherry.

Cherries.

Somewhere in the back of her mind, Sophia remembered something about an annual cherry blossom festival in Georgia. She logged on to the computer again and quickly did a search.

According to the website, the International Cherry Blossom Festival was held in Macon, Georgia, each year near the end of March. It was a ten-day-long celebration that featured food, rides, concerts, a pink pancake breakfast and even movies in the park. It was a big deal for the city. She found the logo for the event and then pulled up the video of her sister pleading for her life. The logo matched the sticker that was on the box behind Kylie, and it was this year's logo, not the one used for previous events.

So, what did that mean? Had the owner of the place where they were holding Kylie bought something for the festival that was stored in the boxes? Or was the owner storing something that was being readied to ship to the festival organizers?

She looked closer at the box but still didn't see any other helpful information. The box was nondescript, with no shipping label or visible markings. There was packing tape sealing the seams shut, but there was nothing unusual about it.

Sophia went back to the festival website and looked for the sponsors list. There were fifteen gold corporate sponsors and about thirty silver corporate sponsors. It was time-consuming, but she started at the top and looked into each of the sponsors, hoping that one of them was based in or near Flint Rock, Georgia. She was assuming that Kylie was being held in a warehouse for a sponsoring company. She had no idea if her assumption was correct, but she had to start somewhere, and the quest had given her a second wind.

Her fingers flew over the keys as she dug into the research.

After an hour, she went in search of the coffeepot. She filled two cups, grabbed some napkins and cream and sugar, remembering how Noah had fixed his coffee at her apartment the day before, and returned to the conference room.

Noah entered the conference room soon after, yawning and rubbing the sleep from his eyes. She handed him the coffee, placed a Danish on a napkin and handed him that, too. He wolfed the pastry down in three quick bites. She laughed, got him another and then took one for herself.

"Hungry?" She smiled as she took a seat by his. Her eyes were crossing after so much time on the computer. It was as good a time as any to take a short break.

"Starving." He took another bite, followed it with a swig of coffee and made a face. "I recognize the horrible precinct coffee we always have, but who brought in the Danish? These aren't half bad."

Sophia shrugged. "I don't know. They just showed up on the table when I went to the bathroom. If I had to guess, I think it was Roman who brought them. He was sleeping at his desk when I first woke up, but then he disappeared."

Noah had a smear of icing from the pastry on his chin. She raised her hand, intending to brush it away, but stopped herself. What was she thinking? She quickly dropped her hand and busied herself with eating her own Danish. She could feel Noah's eyes on her, but she avoided looking at him as she took a bite and stirred a packet of sugar into her coffee. The air felt charged with electricity. She needed to move. Now.

Standing, she went back over to sit in front of the laptop she'd been searching from. But she kept missing the keys as she typed. Why was there suddenly no air to breathe in this room?

She needed a diversion and quickly. Something, anything, to make her stop thinking about kissing Noah Bradley.

"I found something this morning," she murmured softly. "The sticker on the box behind Kylie in the video is from the International Cherry Blossom Festival they hold in Macon each year. I've been researching the different companies that sponsor the event, but so far, I haven't found any connections to the case." She felt Noah come up behind her, and the air became even more electrified. A shiver went down her spine. Was he as affected as she was? She was afraid to glance at him to find out.

Without a word, he touched her shoulders and kneaded them softly. She closed her eyes and enjoyed the contact, the warmth from his hands giving her comfort and a peaceful feeling she hadn't experienced in a long time. She was surprised to realize that she welcomed his touch, when only a couple of days ago she had stiffened and pulled away. She had seen such a different side to him as they had worked together. The new Noah had matured and become a man that she was proud to know.

"If that room where they are holding Kylie is in a warehouse, then there could certainly be a connection to the festival," Noah replied softly.

Sophia found herself leaning into his hands. She just couldn't help herself. "I made a big assumption by hoping that my sister was being held somewhere near Flint Rock. I was hoping that one of the sponsors had a connection with that part of Georgia." Did her voice sound as breathless to Noah as it did to her own ears? Good grief, what was wrong with her?

"Hey, who ate all my Danish?" Roman said as he entered the conference room. He went straight to the open box and looked inside as Noah dropped his hands and took a step back. Sophia's shoulders felt immediately bereft.

"We saved you a couple," Noah replied with a smile. "Thanks for bringing those in, by the way. I was really hungry."

Roman raised an eyebrow, then broke out into a smile. It was obvious that in the short time that had elapsed, he had gone somewhere, taken a shower, shaved, and was now impeccably dressed. His pants even appeared ironed, as they had a perfect crease down the front. He was carrying a gym bag, and he tossed it to Noah, who caught it in the air.

"Here's something else for you. I grabbed my go bag out of the trunk. We're about the same size, so those clothes should work." He gave Noah a sly grin. "Now maybe you'll be decently dressed for the office."

Noah laughed and unzipped the bag. Sophia could just see a shaving kit and a set of clothing. She remembered Noah had left a similar bag at her apartment last night, and it was probably right where they'd left it, sitting by the couch. She wondered how often an investigation had these detectives working around the clock like this one. It must be rather frequently if they prepared enough to keep a go bag on hand on a regular basis.

Her respect for them, and for law enforcement in general, went up another notch. She wondered if the general public knew how dedicated these people really were to protecting and serving their communities. At a moment's notice, they were ready to go, and they didn't leave with a job half done. They kept on pushing until the goal was accomplished. Their work ethic was inspiring.

"Thanks, Roman. I owe you one." Noah's voice seemed a bit husky, but Sophia still couldn't look at him. Her feelings were too jumbled.

Roman shrugged and took another bite of his Danish as Noah filled him in on what Sophia had researched about the festival.

Roman sat at the laptop he had been using and pulled up one of his police databases. "This program might speed up the search. What are the common terms you are using?"

She went over the various searches she had already performed. "I haven't found any leads so far," Sophia admitted, "but I'm only about halfway through the silver list. There weren't any hits on the gold list."

"It's a good idea," Roman commented as his fingers flew over the keys. "You keep working on that list. I'll start on suppliers."

"And I'll go clean up and make myself presentable," Noah said as he shouldered the gym bag and headed for the door. "Sophia, I'm sure we can scare up a toothbrush for you, if you're in need of one."

"Thanks, but I have one." She had learned long ago to carry around a few toiletries in her bag, just in case. She finally looked up at him. He gave her a smile, then left the room.

She returned to her keyboard and moved on to the next name on her list, glad that the feelings of attraction had at least dissipated long enough for her to focus on her research again. She wasn't sure what to make of those feelings, and right now, she didn't want to analyze them too closely.

A half hour later, Roman pushed his chair back. "Found it!" he exclaimed, excitement in his voice.

Noah returned, clean-shaved and wearing a new set of khakis with a white shirt and a teal paisley tie. He sheepishly claimed the last Danish and came up behind Roman so he could see his screen. Sophia also leaned over to take a look, Roman's excitement making her own anticipation spike.

"Southern Imports, Incorporated, sells fireworks to vendors all over the region, including the International Cherry Blossom Festival." Roman smiled and tapped a few more keys. He looked like the Cheshire cat. "Guess who owns the company?"

THIRTEEN

"John Prensky!" Sophia exclaimed as she read the name from the screen. "And, look, he has a warehouse in Albany, Georgia. That's just a hop, skip and jump from Flint Rock!"

Roman pushed back his chair. "Yep." He looked up at Noah. "According to this, his company sells a lot more than just fireworks, like party supplies, banners—the whole enchilada. Based on these pictures, he has a warehouse and office space at the same location on the western side of Albany. How do you want to handle it?"

"Charlie is already down in Flint Rock," Noah responded. "He started working with the local boys yesterday. Can you get the warrant? While you're working on that, I can coordinate the search." He pulled out his cell phone as Roman nodded and quickly left the room.

Noah turned back to Sophia, dialing as he

spoke. "And while we're doing that, can you dig into Southern Imports? I want to know everything there is to know about that company, especially the names of the officers, other shareholders, major customers... You know—all of it. I doubt John Prensky did the kidnapping all by himself. In fact, I'm sure he didn't because he had an alibi that we've already verified, and he couldn't have been in two places at one time. He must have had help."

Sophia nodded and turned back to her computer. Her heart was beating like a bass drum against her rib cage as the excitement built. Were they finally close to finding Kylie? Hope surged within her.

After reading about the company through the website pages, she turned to the county clerk's office and the state government sites to locate the incorporation papers and any other information she could find. She could hear Noah in the background, working with Charlie and the local police department as they developed a plan to approach the warehouse.

A few minutes later, he was talking to Roman and a clerk at the courthouse. The search warrant was issued and sent to the authorities in Flint Rock. Everything seemed to be going smoothly so far. She turned back to her laptop and typed furiously, then froze as a name came across the screen.

She glanced over at Noah, her heart in her throat. Noah was walking back and forth at the end of the conference table, talking to someone on his cell about the search warrant. When he saw Sophia's reaction, he hastily ended the call and came to her side.

"What's wrong?"

Sophia pointed to her screen. "What was the name of that sergeant from the ASU police department who was searching for Sophia?"

"Kittinger, I think. Why?"

"Do you know his first name?"

"No, but it's easy enough to find out." He leaned over her screen. "What are we looking at?"

"These are the incorporation papers for Southern Imports." Sophia pointed to a list of names. "These are the officers. If Esau Kittinger is the same man that works for the campus police, I think I know why nobody has found Kylie yet. He's probably working with John Prensky. He's one of the kidnappers!"

Noah squeezed her shoulder and quickly

made another call. "Roman, we've got a problem." He went on to describe what Sophia had found and asked him to obtain a warrant to search Sergeant Kittinger's office and home, as well as an arrest warrant for the man himself. Then he called Charlie and updated him on the entire situation.

Sophia stood and hugged herself, pacing as Noah handled the details of coordinating the search. She suddenly felt nauseous. What if they were too late? What if Kylie was already dead? Fear and doubt assailed her and made her hands shake. She grabbed her elbows, trying to stop the involuntary movements, and took a deep breath, hoping she could settle her nerves.

Noah finally hung up and moved quickly to Sophia's side. He held out his arms while tilting his head and beckoning with his eyes, giving her the choice.

Sophia didn't hesitate. She stepped willingly into his embrace, savoring the warmth and comfort he was offering. It felt so good to just be held. It made her feel safe, as if all of the heartache she was experiencing was actually surmountable.

"It's going to be okay," Noah murmured. "You did great investigative work. Now let

Charlie and his team exercise the warrants. We should hear something soon. Charlie is good at his job. He knows what he's doing."

"What if she's dead?" Sophia whispered against his shirt. "What if they killed her right after they sent that video?"

"They wouldn't do that," Noah reassured her. "They haven't gotten what they want yet. She's still leverage to them. That means she has value. They're not going to throw that away. Don't give up."

Sophia felt the tears threaten, yet wasn't able to stop them. "Noah, I'm so scared." She could feel herself trembling, but she couldn't stop that, either. Noah gently rubbed his hand on her back, and the motion helped soothe her apprehension, as did the spicy scent of his aftershave, but it wasn't enough to stop the crying. For several minutes, he held her as she cried. When the tears finally slowed, she was spent, exhaustion and stress overwhelming her.

"Remember when we were twelve and we got caught in that storm near the lake? We hid under the tree for a while, but even though the rain slowed, we still got completely soaked before the day was over."

The memory was a sweet one, and a very

good distraction. She could see them both as children in her mind's eye, back by the lake, laughing under that tree.

"Yes, I remember," Sophia whispered. "I was afraid of the thunder, but you kept making up stories about what was causing it. I think my favorite was you said God was bowling, and the really loud booms were when he made a strike."

Noah rested his head on hers, pulling her even closer. "And after the thunder passed, do you remember what we did?"

Sophia gave a small smile. She couldn't help herself. "Sure. You had been begging me to teach you how to dance because you wanted to take me to the sixth-grade spring party. We spent the next two hours practicing."

"I was so awful!" Noah exclaimed. "And you were extremely patient. I think I must have stepped on your feet about fifty times, but you kept at it."

"Well, I couldn't have you tripping all over yourself in front of the other guys. You would have been embarrassed, and then you wouldn't have taken me to another dance ever again."

"I saw that painting on the wall in your

apartment of a couple ballroom dancing. Do you still like to dance?" Noah asked quietly.

"I love it. I was in the ballroom dance club in college, and I still go to organized dances when I get a chance. The waltz is my favorite, but there are several dances that I enjoy. The mambo is a lot of fun, and I even like salsa."

Noah swayed with Sophia and moved his hands into new positions as if dancing with her. One hand encircled her waist and held her close; the other took her right hand. "When this is all over, I'll take you dancing, just like old times. I promise not to step on your toes."

Sophia leaned back slightly so she could see his eyes. He was serious. "Do you know how to dance?" she asked.

"I took a few classes, but I'm sure I'm nowhere near as good as you. I was in Matthews's wedding party last year, and five or six of us learned a few steps so we could dance at his reception. I know just enough to be dangerous."

She gave a small laugh and leaned her head against his shoulder. He had done the impossible in a difficult situation. He had distracted her for a moment and reminded her of good times long gone.

"Thank you, Noah." She stepped back

from his embrace and happened to glance at the nearby trash can. She laughed when she saw the wrappers of four different packs of Doublemint gum at the bottom. He was a new man in her eyes, but some things never changed.

Roman came in just as Sophia was returning to her computer. He went straight to the laptop connected to the LCD and started typing.

Noah raised an eyebrow and glanced over his shoulder at the screen. "Something new?" he asked, hopeful.

He was glad that he hadn't been holding Sophia when Roman had entered the room. He'd already been on the receiving end of several pointed looks and raised eyebrows from Roman and some of his other colleagues, but thankfully, no one had made him explain their relationship yet. He wasn't even sure what he would say if he were asked.

We were childhood friends, but I totally blew it by not apologizing sooner and wasted the last nine years of my life without her?

I fell in love with her back in high school, and now all of those old feelings are coming back and she's all I can think about?

I can't breathe unless she's near me?

It was true. How was he going to go on without her in his life after this case was over? He loved her. In fact, his feelings had been growing exponentially ever since she had walked into his office. She was allowing him to comfort her, which was progress. But did she feel anything for him beyond friendship? He had absolutely no idea. And he couldn't talk to her about it, especially with her sister missing. He stretched his arms out along his sides, missing the feel of holding Sophia close to his heart. Focus. He had to stay focused on this case. He forced his thoughts back to Kylie and the operation in Flint Rock.

Roman hit a few more keys, and a video came to life on the LCD. It showed a group of officers, guns drawn, going into a small house. "This is the strike team entering Esau Kittinger's house to arrest him. He's probably not home, since his car wasn't in the driveway. They couldn't find him at work, though, so they had to try. He seems to have disappeared."

Sophia sat in the chair by Roman and kept her eyes glued on the screen. The officers announced themselves and entered the house.

They cleared each room of the residence before the leader's voice came through the speaker. "He's not here. Looks like our bird has flown the coop. We'll put an APB out for him and his vehicles immediately."

Noah nodded, realizing that the all-points bulletin was the best way to find the missing officer. He saw that Roman had opened a channel so that they could talk to the strike team leader. "Thanks for letting us join in. If you find him, let us know."

"You got it," the leader responded. Then he clicked a button on his vest camera and the video and audio feed both disappeared.

"Okay," Roman said quietly as he punched a few more keys. "The other team is almost ready to breach the warehouse. They'll be connecting to our computer in a moment, and we'll be able to watch that raid, too."

"How does this work?" Sophia asked.

"The laptop connects to a program in the officer's body cam. It's almost like having a GoPro camera and a police radio all in one that's attached to the officer's chest. They can't hear us unless he purposefully lets us. It's better that way so we don't make a noise and ruin the operation by mistake. But once he clicks in, we can have a conversation as well as video."

The picture suddenly flickered and they could see another group of officers readying to enter the warehouse. They used hand signals to communicate as they moved into position. Then, as soon as everyone was in the correct location, they breached, shouting "Law enforcement!" as they entered. The officers quickly spread out and began searching the building.

The warehouse was empty.

Noah's heart sank as the officer's body cam turned full circle to show the viewers the warehouse. Several shelves, filled with boxes of varying shapes, lined the walkways, as well as forklifts and stacks of crates. They could hear officers yelling "Clear!" as other areas of the warehouse were secured. So far, not a single person was anywhere in the building.

"Have them look for an office or other room where they could have been holding her," Noah requested, his eyes studying everything, even the smallest detail, in the warehouse.

Roman relayed the command, and the leader made his way through the aisles until he came to a row of three offices. Two were quickly searched and cleared. Nothing.

The third held a desk, a chair, and a large bookcase filled with binders against the back wall. The side wall was lined with a stack of boxes of varying sizes. Some had International Cherry Blossom Festival stickers on them; others weren't labeled. In the middle of the room was the chair where Kylie had been tied during the video. The bindings lay on the floor and the chair was empty, almost seeming to mock them.

They were too late. Kylie was gone, along with her abductors.

Noah's jaw clenched as his chest tightened. They had missed her. But the day's search wasn't a total loss. Now, at least, they knew who'd taken Kylie and why. He looked over at Sophia and hoped she could read the regret and sorrow in his eyes.

His cell phone rang and he took the call. After a few short answers, he hung up and stored his phone.

"That was the prosecutor at the courthouse. The defense just rested. Arlo Prensky's case just got sent to the jury."

FOURTEEN

"Kittinger is not at the courthouse," Roman confirmed, his call on Noah's speakerphone. "We really didn't expect him to show up there, but we had John Prensky under surveillance in case they met up. Now he has disappeared, as well." He ended the call.

Sophia sat motionless, numbly taking in all that was going on around her. Warrants had been issued for John Prensky's home and office in Atlanta, but a search of each location had proved fruitless. How could people disappear so easily in this day and age?

"How did Kittinger know to move my sister? Did someone warn him?"

Noah nodded, his face grim. "A clerk that worked for the judge in Flint Rock gave him the heads-up as soon as the judge signed the warrant. She and Kittinger are friends, and they are probably dating. In any case, she gave him a call about twenty minutes before we searched the warehouse. She's under arrest and isn't talking. Her first words when we tried to interrogate her were 'Get me a lawyer.'"

Sophia absorbed this new information. She was done crying. Now she was angry. "So Kittinger was lying all this time about trying to find Kylie?"

"Yes. Looks like he and John Prensky were childhood friends. They grew up together. They apparently remained friends and even became business partners over the years. In fact, Kittinger owns an interest in Prensky's fireworks business, and he manages some of the sales to the festival organizers and such on the side."

Sophia shook her head, remembering how Noah had expressed misgivings about Kittinger earlier in the investigation. "Looks like your gut was right all along."

Roman looked up from his computer. "We're not sunk yet. Esau Kittinger is driving an older-model car that doesn't have a GPS system, but John Prensky has a newer Toyota. I'm working with Toyota now to get the data. Give me a minute, and we'll be ready to go find his car."

"Good work," Noah said before turning. "Sophia, let's go get you a bulletproof vest. We need to pack up and be ready to go as soon as we find his location. I'm guessing he's still in the Atlanta area since he was so invested in watching the trial. Now that it's gone to the jury, I'm thinking he and Kittinger are going to meet up somewhere to decide what to do about Kylie. All we need is a location, and we'll be good to go."

She followed him out of the conference room and down the hallway to a storage room filled with gear of all shapes and sizes. He got his own vest that had his name inside, then pulled one of the spares from the shelf, checked the size and handed it to her. "Try this one."

She pulled it over her head, and he helped her with the straps, checking to make sure it fit her correctly.

"That'll do," he said softly. He looked up and met her eyes. "We're going to find her, Sophia. Have faith." He leaned forward and gave her a chaste kiss on the forehead. "We're going to do everything we can to save your sister."

Sophia nodded, unable to speak. Despite the anxiety that kept coming at her in waves, she knew without a doubt that Noah meant what he said, and that his entire team was committed to finding Kylie. She held his sea-blue eyes and studied him for a moment. Gone was the rowdy, self-absorbed teenager she had known. In his place stood an honorable man who had done his utmost to help. In fact, he had even put his own life on the line to find Kylie.

Her respect for him went up another notch. No one could promise a positive outcome, but Sophia knew instinctively that if Kylie did have to pay the ultimate price, Noah would stay by her side to help her through it.

She reached out and cupped his cheek with her hand. "Thank you, Noah. You've been amazing. I couldn't have asked for more."

She also said a silent prayer, thanking God, as well, for bringing Noah into her life during this desperate time. She had gotten his help, and she had also put to rest some of the difficulties from her past. Maybe they could actually be friends after this was all over. After all, God was the God of second chances, wasn't He?

Noah covered her hand with his own. "You are very welcome." He gave her a reassuring smile before his expression turned serious.

"I don't want you in the line of fire when we find Prensky and Kittinger, but I want to take you with us in case Kylie is there. That way, you can see her right away and comfort her while we process everything. Will you promise me you'll stay in the car until after we've made the arrest? I hate making you wait, but I really don't want you hurt. I also don't want to be forced to leave you behind if you don't agree."

Sophia nodded, thankful that he'd considered her safety as well as what would be best for Kylie. It also saved her the trouble of arguing with him. She had always planned to go—even if she'd had to follow from behind in her own vehicle. She looked into his eyes and could tell that he had anticipated her move and had outmaneuvered her, but she didn't care. As long as she got to be there when they found Kylie, nothing else mattered. "I'll stay in the car. I promise."

He squeezed her hand, then brought it to his lips and kissed the inside of her palm. "Let's go. Roman will have an address for us soon. We want to be ready."

Sophia followed him out of the room, her heart pounding. She glanced at her hand where he had kissed her and bent her fingers, as if to hold on to the kiss before it escaped. Why had he kissed her? That was twice in about five minutes. Both kisses had been friendly without being forward or suggestive, but they still made her wonder. How did he feel about her? And how did she feel about him? Her thoughts churned as she walked.

They returned to the conference room, where Matthews had joined Roman and they were going over the details of the upcoming operation. Roman looked up and shared the news.

"Backup is ready. We roll in five. We have an address on the southwest side of town near the airport. John Prensky's car is at a house that belongs to his cousin. We're hoping to find him there, too."

"Let me run the op," Noah said roughly, his tone leaning toward the demanding side.

Roman shook his head. When he spoke, his tone was equally resolute. "Not a chance, Noah. Be glad I'm even letting you come along." He lowered his voice, but Sophia could still hear his words. "I've seen how you look at her. We all have. You either do it my way or you don't do it at all."

Matthews, standing behind Roman, crossed his arms. It was clear he agreed with Roman.

Noah's eyes went back and forth between his two colleagues. He glanced at Sophia, then finally put up his hands in a motion of surrender. "All right, all right. You've got this."

Roman nodded, his expression intense. "Yes, I do."

Noah shifted and adjusted his vest a little to the left, waiting for the signal. He stood partially hidden by the side of the house, ready to back up the other officers once they entered.

He glanced over at Roman, who flanked the front door with Matthews. A third officer, standing slightly behind Roman, carried a battering ram to breach the door if needed. Two other officers flanked the back door, and another officer, opposite Noah, watched the far side of the house. They had the building surrounded. Prensky's expensive burgundy 4Runner was parked out by the curb. All signs pointed to Prensky being in the house. The question was, would Kittinger and Kylie be with him?

Roman stepped out of the line of fire, then reached over and knocked. When no one answered, he tried the knob and found the door locked, despite the fact that they could hear someone moving around inside. "Police! Open up!" He waited about ten seconds and then nodded to the officer to breach the door. "Police! Freeze!"

Noah ran up the porch stairs and entered behind his colleagues, his gun trained on John Prensky, who had dropped his weapon and raised his hands when Roman and Matthews had entered the house. His face was a mixture of anger and humiliation, fire shooting from his eyes as he glared at the intruders.

Noah heard other cops calling out as they cleared the rest of the home and his heart sank.

Kittinger and Kylie were nowhere to be found.

"Where's Kylie?" Noah demanded as Roman secured Prensky's gun and read him his Miranda rights. Prensky said nothing as he was handcuffed and frisked to verify that there were no other weapons hidden somewhere on his body.

Noah took a step forward and repeated the question. This time Prensky looked up with a smirk. His body language and attitude were clearly very different from when they had interviewed him at the courthouse. This time, he knew the jig was up, and defiance filled his countenance.

"Kylie who?" Prensky said flippantly. He allowed the search and didn't change his expression. In fact, if anything, he stood proudly, his back ramrod-straight, his demeanor insolent. His lip curled when he spoke, and anger seemed to radiate from his entire being. "I have no idea what or who you're talking about."

Noah advanced quickly, his own body language so threatening that Prensky actually took a step back. "In case you haven't figured it out yet, we're not playing games here. Now you need to make a decision. Do you want to spend a few years in prison or the rest of your natural-born life behind bars? It makes no difference to me. I'll find the girl either way. But if you want to help yourself, now is the time."

"Go ahead and arrest me," Prensky spit. "You're good at arresting the wrong guy. Why stop now? I've got proof Arlo never killed that woman. You just never wanted to believe it."

"So, your answer was to kidnap an innocent girl? Terrorize her and make her live with the trauma for the rest of her life?" Noah holstered his gun and fisted his hands. "If you've got proof, all you had to do was bring it to the police. We would have listened and investigated whatever you brought us, but you never darkened our door. I never even laid eyes on you before the trial. You have nothing. But even if you did, kidnapping isn't the answer. It isn't the way to get people to do what you want when you think you were treated unfairly."

"As if you would have cared if I'd brought you something exculpatory," Prensky accused. "You just chose the path of least resistance and arrested the first man you came across."

"As I testified to in court, Arlo Prensky's DNA was all over the crime scene."

"Which could have been planted."

"I'm not that kind of cop."

"Sure you are."

Noah gritted his teeth, but Roman pushed him to the side and got between the two men.

"We know you've been working with Esau Kittinger," Roman said tightly. "We've got your phone records. We know you teamed up to kidnap Kylie Archer to use her to blackmail Sophia Archer into trying to prove Arlo's innocence. We found where you were holding her in your warehouse in Albany. It won't take us long to put the rest of this case together, and when we do, we won't be interested in making any kind of deal with you."

Roman took a step closer so their faces were mere inches apart. "We're fighting the clock on this one, Prensky, so you can either tell us what we want to know, or we can take you straight over to booking. Like the detective said, we're not playing games with you. Tell us where to find Kittinger and Kylie. Now. Help us save her life, and we'll help save yours."

Prensky eyed Roman before his eyes moved over to Noah and then back.

He tried to maintain his bravado, but the fear of going to prison must have finally sunk in. He wilted and threw back his head. "Okay. Fine. But you have to realize, I only did this because my nephew is innocent. He's family and I had to step in. I know he's not perfect. I get that. But there's no way he would've ever killed that woman. He's not a murderer."

Prensky's voice turned emphatic as he tried to convince them. "It was wrong to kidnap Kylie. I see that now. She's innocent, too. I never should have done that, and I never should have involved Kittinger. I was so desperate I just wasn't thinking straight. We wouldn't have hurt her. I promise you." He looked over at Noah again. "We just wanted someone from the outside to reinvestigate the case, someone we knew would be motivated to do a good job. Some of my cousins have been following Sophia ever since I made that call to tell her about the kidnapping. We knew she'd take the investigation seriously and really look into that student's murder, not just go through the motions. We were going to release Kylie after the verdict was issued, no matter what."

"Well, if you wanted her to investigate so badly, why did you lock us in that basement office at the university?" Noah asked caustically.

"I didn't!" Prensky denied, his eyes widening. "We couldn't figure out what had happened to you in there. We saw you go in, but then hours later you came out on stretchers. We couldn't figure out what had occurred. Then I sent someone over to the hospital to find out what had happened. I didn't have anything to do with that gas leak. I promise." His shoulders slumped. "I never would have hurt either of you or Kylie. I just wanted Arlo exonerated. He's family, and I know he's innocent. He didn't murder that student. It just isn't possible. He isn't capable of hurting anyone."

"Well, are you?" Noah asked. "That's the real question here. Someone has tried to kill us both on multiple occasions ever since we started looking into the case again. What about the bombing at Maggie Spencer's apartment? Three people died in that attack."

"I didn't do that, either! I didn't want you dead. I wanted Ms. Archer to investigate the case, and I wanted you to see your mistake. Period. How am I going to get Arlo freed if you're poisoned or killed in a bombing?" Prensky swallowed hard. "I don't know who planted that bomb. I don't even know the first thing about how to make one."

"You sell fireworks, don't you?" Roman asked.

Prensky shrugged. "Sure I do. But that's a far cry from buying a bomb that brings down an entire building. I don't even make the fireworks. I just buy them wholesale and resell them." He narrowed his eyes, which were going back and forth between the two cops. When he spoke, his voice was almost fanatical. "Arlo is innocent. He didn't murder that woman. After everything you've been investigating, surely you must know that."

"His DNA was at the crime scene," Noah said under his breath. It always came back to that fact. "His blood was all over the victim. Sometimes, people use drugs or get drunk and do things you wouldn't think possible. The evidence pointed to him and him alone."

"Then the DNA had to have been planted. Please, listen to reason."

Roman took Prensky's arm roughly and started pulling him toward the door. "Enough. Tell us what we want to know about Kylie and Kittinger, or we're done."

Prensky dragged his feet, pulling against Roman's grip. "Look, if Arlo had committed the murder, Maggie's computer would have surfaced by now. Arlo doesn't even know how to use a computer. He would have hocked that thing before the night was over. He was so strapped for cash, he would have pawned it or sold it immediately. You checked all the pawnshops, right? You didn't find it. Arlo isn't the sharpest knife in the drawer. If he'd sold it, you would have found it."

Noah put his hands on his hips. "We don't have time to rehash Arlo's case any longer. The jury will decide his guilt or innocence.

What we need to know is where Kittinger is holding Kylie Archer. That poor girl has been through enough. If you're not going to tell us, then we're done talking."

Once again, Roman started for the door, and once again, Prensky balked. "Okay, okay." Prensky's voice was low, defeated. "But you'll put in a good word for me with the prosecutor, right?"

"Yes," Roman said emphatically. "You have my word."

Noah was glad Roman had agreed. He doubted Prensky would have trusted him to help, but with Roman standing there, exuding authority, they might actually have a chance of getting the truth out of this man.

Prensky grimaced and a muscle twitched in his jaw. "Kittinger has her at my cousin's apartment here in Atlanta. My cousin is out of town and doesn't even know we are using the place. The address is in my phone."

Noah grabbed Prensky's phone from his pocket where he had stored it after they had searched him.

"Passcode?"

"It's 546798."

"What's your cousin's name?"

"Lenny Campbell."

Noah thumbed through Prensky's contacts and stopped at the listing for his cousin. "He lives at 142 Eastern Sky Drive." He got in Prensky's face again. "You'd better hope that they really are there and that Kittinger hasn't hurt Kylie. If you're wrong, or if Kylie even has a broken fingernail, you'll be seeing me again. And soon."

FIFTEEN

Noah, Sophia, Roman and Matthews waited in the car, watching the Campbell residence for any signs of life. They were only a block away, with a good view of the front yard and door. Another car was stationed behind the house and was watching the alleyway, just in case the building was approached from the back.

Unfortunately, the team had already searched the home and found it empty, but after discovering a bag full of clothing and toiletries that seemed to belong to Kittinger, they figured that the kidnapper was only on an errand with the girl and would return momentarily. They had decided a stakeout was the way to go, and they'd left the house as they had found it. Hopefully, Kittinger and Kylie would return soon and an arrest could be made without incident.

A black car drove by, then a red Camaro. Noah kept his eyes peeled, anxious to see if the campus police sergeant would appear. His muscles felt tight, and he stretched a bit, working out the kinks. He couldn't remember ever wanting to solve a case more fervently.

Sophia would survive if her sister was dead, but it would be a very hard road for her. It would change her forever. He didn't wish that kind of pain on anyone and still committed to doing everything he could to find Kylie. He was fairly confident that John Prensky had told them the truth about Esau Kittinger and Kylie's whereabouts, but if not, he wouldn't stop until Sophia's sister was safely back home.

They weren't sure what vehicle the coconspirator was driving, so Noah glanced again at his phone and the Department of Transportation records that showed that Esau Kittinger owned a silver Ford sedan and a black 750 Harley-Davidson motorcycle. Neither vehicle had been found at the house in Flint Rock, so they didn't know which he was using or if he had picked up something else. Either way, Noah carefully studied every car and truck that passed, just in case.

Noah was also holding a photo of Kittinger that he'd found on the internet so they could verify they had the right man before completing the arrest. The photo was of Kittinger's graduation from the law enforcement academy, and he was wearing his dress Flint Rock University campus police uniform, the United States flag behind him. He sported a wide smile that showed a row of perfect white teeth and a small dimple in his left cheek. Noah wanted to wipe that smug smile off the man's face himself. He couldn't imagine why a cop would break the law and kidnap a young girl—even to appease a friend. Kittinger had taken an oath to protect and serve, and he had violated that promise in the worst way possible.

A large van drove by, and Noah gritted his teeth in frustration. They'd already been there an hour and a half. Surely, Kittinger would arrive soon. He tapped his hand against his thigh, anxious to get this show on the road.

He glanced over at Sophia, who was quiet and pensive. To her credit, she was holding it together amazingly well. He wanted to touch her, to reassure her, but he didn't know if she would welcome it. He also didn't dare to reach out while Roman and Matthews were in the car. Both fellow officers had already voiced their concern about his involvement with Sophia. There was no reason to make their suspicions worse. He knew he was walking a fine line between being too invested and remaining objective, but he was glad that his colleagues were willing to give him the benefit of the doubt while he figured things out.

And he needed to figure things out.

What would he do if Sophia decided to limit their relationship to friendship alone? He'd reacted poorly the last time he had been rejected. He knew he would handle it better this time. But it would still break his heart. He loved this woman. He now knew that without a doubt. Sophia was a class act that no one could follow, and he couldn't imagine his life without her, especially now that he had been given a second chance.

But he couldn't force her to share his feelings, and he definitely didn't want to try. If friendship was all that was offered, he would just have to accept it. Noah also knew he wanted to help reunite her with her sister, whether she loved him or not. And he would always be thankful that God had given him the opportunity to ask for forgiveness and put the past to rest.

Noah noticed the small stress lines around

Sophia's eyes and mouth. She noticed his glance and gave him a small smile in return. Even when going through one of the most difficult times in her life, she radiated kindness and caring. She was simply a beautiful person, inside and out.

He knew God had a plan for him; he was sure of it, and the Bible told him so, as well, in several passages. If that plan included Sophia, it would be wonderful, but if it didn't, then God would see him through and help him deal with the loss. He had to trust God to know what and who was best for him. It was easier said than done sometimes, but Noah realized deep down that he was only able to see a small part of the picture, while God saw the entire canvas. He was creating a beautiful work in Noah's life, with or without Sophia.

Noah took a deep breath and turned his thoughts back to the case.

A white Honda Civic passed by as he studied the house again, anxiousness making his muscles tense.

Dear God, please help us find Kylie safe and sound, he prayed silently.

Suddenly a motorcycle roared past, a male driving and a female seated behind him. Both were wearing helmets, so their identities couldn't be verified, but all four occupants of the car sat taller and watched as the bike pulled up to Campbell's garage, stopped and parked. It was a Harley and the right color, but who were the riders?

"All units get ready to move," Roman commanded through his police radio.

The girl got off the bike first, but she was holding her hands in an awkward way. As Noah studied them, he could tell that they were zip-tied together. Then the man got off and pocketed the key. He took off his helmet and then turned to the girl and removed hers. Brown hair cascaded down the girl's back, and she shook her head, moving her hands clumsily to push a lock behind her ear.

"That's Kylie!" Sophia exclaimed.

"And that's Kittinger," Noah added.

"Targets identified," Roman said into his radio. "Move in now!"

All three cops got out of the car, but Noah was fastest. He ran straight for Kittinger, who had his back to the police officers who were advancing. He turned just as Noah tackled him and pressed him up against the outside wall of the house. Kittinger groaned as the air was forced from his lungs, and Kylie screamed, not knowing what was going on.

She moved back and barely missed being hit by Kittinger's flailing arms as he struggled to escape. Matthews was quick to pull her out of harm's way as the two men fought, and Roman had his gun pulled and ready, the barrel trained on the kidnapper.

Noah grabbed Kittinger's arms and threw him to the ground face-first, then straddled his back. The two helmets that Kittinger had been holding went bouncing harmlessly down the driveway as he struggled to free himself from Noah's grip, but Noah was stronger and more determined. He pulled Kittinger's right arm behind his back and forced it upward, then leaned down and pressed against his back, forcing the young officer to stop bucking and fighting.

"Freeze, Kittinger!" Roman roared as he moved to make sure the kidnapper could see that they meant business. "You're done." The Flint Rock policeman saw the metal flash and finally quit fighting. Noah secured his wrists with his handcuffs and pushed away from him, leaving him on the ground.

Noah turned and cut Kylie's hands free from the zip tie just as Sophia ran up to the group and bear-hugged her sister. Within moments, both women were crying.

* * *

Kylie was alive! Sophia could barely control her exuberance. She said a quick prayer of thanksgiving, praising God for keeping her sister safe, then pulled back and held Kylie's face in her hands. She had to look at her and take in every nuance of every feature. She had been so scared that she would never see Kylie again that her relief was palpable. "Are you okay?"

Tears streamed down Kylie's face. Her wide brown eyes had dark circles underneath and her skin was pale and sallow, but she nodded. "I will be."

Sophia pulled her close again, then tried to turn her so she couldn't see Kittinger being taken away from the scene. "You're safe now. That man is never going to hurt you again."

"He was a cop!" Kylie said bitterly as she turned and purposefully watched him being led away in handcuffs. "He was wearing his university law enforcement uniform when he came up to me after class. He said there had been a robbery at the dorms and he needed me to come with him to see if any of the stolen items that they had recovered belonged to me. He told me one big fat lie after another."

"I'm so sorry. Not all cops are like that, though. Do you remember Noah Bradley?"

Kylie sniffed and wiped her eyes. "He was that guy who used to be your friend and then treated you like trash in high school, right?"

"Yeah, that's the guy," Sophia agreed. "But he's changed. I know we didn't end things on a good note, but he's more than made up for it over the last few days. He's been working around the clock to help me find you."

Kylie leaned closer, studying her sister's face. Finally, she gave Sophia a knowing smile. "So, it's like that, huh?"

Sophia frowned, wondering what her sister was seeing. "Like what?"

Kylie leaned closer so only her sister could hear her. "You like him. I can tell." She raised an eyebrow, but when Sophia purposefully didn't react, the younger girl shrugged. "Never mind. I'm so messed up, I don't know if I'm coming or going. I'll tease you after I've had a nap and something to eat. Just forget what I said. Want to get a burger and fries?"

Sophia put her arm around Kylie's shoulders. She was glad the conversation had turned away from Noah. She didn't know how she felt, and now wasn't the time to try to figure it out. Besides, she was too elated that her sister had been found safe and sound to think about anything else. "How about a big, fat, juicy hamburger with fries *and* a chocolate milkshake. Sound good?"

"That sounds wonderful. I hope you have cash. Kittinger took my backpack. I think he threw it away, and it held two books that I need for class and my wallet."

"Not to worry. We'll get you new books and anything else you need." Sophia had to smile. It was so like Kylie to immediately start thinking about the practical things like books and school supplies. She loved that about her sister, but her own mind wasn't ready to close this case and move on quite yet. She was still caught up in the investigation. Although they had answered the questions surrounding Kylie's disappearance, there were still mysteries abounding. Who had tried to kill them besides Maggie's fiancé?

She was still struggling with the questions when Noah approached. He had a hesitant look upon his face, as if he couldn't decide whether or not to interrupt them. Finally, he took a few more steps closer and looked at Kylie from head to toe. "I'm so glad we found you safe and sound."

Sophia gave him a smile as she introduced him. "Kylie, this is Detective Bradley. He's the one who helped save your life."

Kylie shook his hand and gave him a smile. "Thanks for everything you did."

Noah nodded. "You're welcome. Wow, you've sure grown. The last time I saw you, you were still in elementary school."

"I'm in college now," she said proudly.

Sophia laughed at her sister's boast, but Noah just pursed his lips and smiled. "I always knew you'd do great things," he said lightly. "Look, I know you two want to talk, but there are some things we have to do before you start putting this all behind you. First of all, Kylie, we need to get you checked out by a doctor to make sure you're okay after everything you've been through. Do you need me to call an ambulance, or can I drive you to the hospital for an exam?"

Kylie and Sophia exchanged looks. Sophia didn't know everything that had happened to Kylie, but her sister was a smart girl, and she was an adult now. She would know whether or not she needed medical care. Kylie finally shook her head. "I'm okay, and I don't think I need a doctor. I just need some food and some rest."

"Okay. Well, we can definitely get you something to eat, but we need you to come down to the station and file a report so we can get the details from you while they're fresh in your head. I know it's an inconvenience—"

"Oh, no!" Kylie interrupted. "It's not a problem. I'm going to do whatever you need to make sure you punish that man for kidnapping me and whoever else was helping him. That was the scariest thing that has ever happened to me. I want to help."

"Good for you," Noah agreed, obviously relieved that he didn't have to convince her. "The team can finish up here while we head back to the station. What would you like to eat?"

"We've already got a plan," Sophia said with a wink. "Care to drive?"

"Sure thing." His smile lit up his entire face. Sophia felt a twitch of attraction shoot right down to her toes and took a step back, surprised by the sensation. This guy could do toothpaste commercials, she thought fleetingly, he had such a nice smile. She was glad to see him relaxing a bit. For some reason, seeing him this way made her feel warm and contented herself, despite the knowledge that there was more work to do.

It was good to celebrate a win, and finding Kylie definitely fit into the win category. Still, this case was far from over. They needed to discover who had set the bomb that had killed Joanna Crawley, and they needed to find the person who had locked them in the basement at the university.

Noah drove them to the police station, stopping along the way to visit two different drive-through restaurants to get Kylie the exact type of food she had been craving.

Sophia and Noah also bought a meal, despite the danger that was still surrounding them. Sophia was actually hungry for the first time in days. She continued to sip her lemonade as she glanced behind them at the surrounding traffic.

A white sedan was erratically changing lanes and rapidly coming up behind them.

SIXTEEN

"Noah!" Sophia quickly.

"I see it," he said as he maneuvered into another lane. He glanced at his rearview mirror, then in his side mirror as he watched the car approach.

"What's going on?" Kylie asked from the back seat, her voice filling with panic.

"Somebody is following us," Sophia responded, hoping that she could keep the fear from her own voice. "Don't worry. Noah is a good driver."

"Kittinger didn't escape, did he?" Kylie asked, sounding even more terrified.

"No," Noah responded as he sped up and veered around another car. "Kittinger is still in custody. I would have heard about it on the police radio if something had happened. This is somebody else. Somebody with a totally different agenda."

"It could be someone from Prensky's family," Sophia suggested. "The jury is still out."

"You have a point," Noah agreed as he swerved again, this time barely missing a silver minivan that had suddenly slowed in front of them. "But after what happened with Maggie's fiancé, I don't want to take a chance and slow down to ask them." He called in for backup and raced ahead.

Sophia glanced in her own side mirror and then twisted to see behind them. The white automobile, which had fallen farther behind, was still visible. She put her hand behind her seat, and Kylie grabbed it and squeezed.

The girl was terrified, and it was no wonder after what she had just endured. They were getting closer to the police station and Sophia said a prayer that they would make it safely to the building where there was an abundance of armed men and women ready to help. Only a few more blocks to go…

Suddenly the white car veered to the left and disappeared.

"I've got your six," Roman said over the radio, his voice crackling through the static. "I'll stay with the white sedan. You get those ladies to headquarters."

"Copy that," Noah responded. "And thank you."

Sophia took a deep breath as she realized that Roman had heard their call for help and had rushed to their aid. She could hear the sirens as they turned and followed the white vehicle. She released Kylie's hand and turned back in her seat, the relief washing over her. "You guys make quite a team," she said softly as she watched Noah visibly relax and slow his speed. "Roman really helped us out."

"Yep. We're like family, always looking out for each other."

The more she thought about it, the more Sophia agreed with Noah's statement. She hadn't seen Charlie or Matthews much, but even so, they all worked together well and seemed to share a camaraderie that went way beyond mere professionalism.

She contrasted that relationship with the solitary aspects of her own chosen profession. Being a reporter was a lonely business, and she had to view others in her field skeptically if they showed too much interest. More often than not, reporters tried to undercut one another to get a scoop and the prestige that went with it. She'd even had people on her own team try to steal a story from her. She didn't like the cutthroat aspects of the business and, as a result, had opted to work solo for the better part of her career. Seeing what Noah and his team shared gave her pause and made her long for more true connections in her life. With a start, she realized she lived a rather solitary existence and had few people in her life that she could truly count on as friends.

Had she pushed people away in her quest for journalistic integrity?

Had her job become more important than the people around her?

Had she pushed others away because she was afraid of being hurt?

Sophia didn't like the answers to her questions and resolved right then and there to make a better effort at reaching out and maintaining her relationships. She wanted to be a successful reporter, but she also wanted to enjoy the people around her. She would get hurt. People weren't perfect. Everyone made mistakes. But this second chance at friendship with Noah had shown her how much she was missing in her life, and she was ready to start remedying the situation from this day forward.

They made it to the police station, and the

first thing they did was return to the conference room where they had already spent so much time over the past few days. The computers and everything else in the room were right where they had left them.

Noah took off his jacket, then took a seat and began the interview with Kylie about her ordeal. He made lots of notes for his report, but there were no new surprises as Kylie responded to his questions.

Kittinger had abducted her and tied her up, given her a few snacks and a water bottle, and forced her to create the video that he had sent. Sophia wasn't minimizing the trauma that her sister had endured, but she shivered as she considered what else could have happened. Thankfully, God had protected Kylie from anything worse during her time in the warehouse.

"The driver got away," Roman announced as he entered the conference room. "It was a woman, though. I'm sure of it."

Noah leaned back in his chair. "Thank you. We made it back in one piece, and that's what matters." He untied his tie, pulled it from around his neck and threw it on the conference room table. Then he undid the top two buttons of his shirt, as if preparing for another long night.

Roman nodded, but it was clear that he was still processing the situation. "The plates were stolen, but I'll run them down. If it hadn't been for this crazy Atlanta traffic, she would be in custody as we speak."

Sophia understood his frustration. Driving in Atlanta was a living nightmare. Any sort of car chase seemed virtually impossible with the clogged highways and side streets, despite what had happened with Maggie's fiancé and his automobile attack.

She thought through what they knew so far. Prensky's relatives and Kittinger were convinced he was innocent, so they had kidnapped Kylie to force Sophia to reinvestigate the case. Now that they had Kylie back, Prensky's family didn't have any reason to follow her to verify that she was looking into the case. Also, Maggie's fiancé, Mason Tucci, had been working on his own. Once arrested after the car crash, he'd been out of the picture. So who was this woman following them in the white sedan?

She thought back over all of the information they had discovered since they'd reopened the case and turned to Noah, her tone thoughtful. "You know, despite all that we have learned, everything hinges on one simple fact—Prensky's DNA being found at the scene."

Roman took a seat as Noah raised his brow. "That's right. There was blood on the victim and splattered around the crime scene. Some belonged to the victim, but the rest was tested and DNA matched to Arlo Prensky. There was even blood under the victim's fingernails. The evidence was irrefutable."

Sophia leaned forward. "So, let's all agree that the lab got it right and it was Prensky's blood. After all, blood work is hard to dispute in court these days. In fact, it's almost impossible, and lab errors are few and far between, especially of this magnitude. So, for the sake of argument, if Arlo didn't murder Maggie Spencer, how else could the blood have gotten there?"

"I don't want to think about it anymore!" Kylie announced as she stood and put her hands over her ears. "I'm tired, and I just want to get away from all of this. I want to go back to the dorms."

The young girl was almost in tears, but Noah was up and out of his chair, reaching her before Sophia did. He embraced Kylie and let her cry. He looked over at Sophia. "I think she's been through enough. But I don't think it's safe to take her back to your apartment yet. Not until we have more answers. She doesn't need to be a part of the rest of the investigation, though. Now that I've interviewed her, she is free to go. Do you want to take her to a hotel?"

Roman stood. "I'll take her home with me," he announced, his voice firm. "My sister, Cindy, is staying with me this week, and she's bored silly. She and Kylie are about the same age, and my home is like a small fortress. She'll be safe while the two of you figure out the rest of this mess, and Cindy will keep her occupied."

Noah glanced over at Sophia to gauge her thoughts. Before she could even voice an opinion, Kylie had pulled away from Noah and was drying her tears with her sleeve. "How old is Cindy?"

"Eighteen," Roman replied. "She finished high school last year and has been working full-time at the local grocery store while she's deciding what to do with her life. Since you're a big college girl, maybe you can give her a nudge in the right direction."

Kylie smiled. "I'd like that." She turned to

Sophia. "I know you need to keep working on this, but I just need some distance. I want to feel normal again, you know?"

"I get it," Sophia agreed. "But are you sure you're okay with going to Roman's house? I can take you to a hotel if that's what you want to do, and I'll stay there with you so you won't be alone."

"No, I'd rather go meet Cindy," Kylie said with a smile. She gave Sophia a playful nudge. "I love you, and I'm really thankful for everything you did to rescue me, but I need a change of scenery so I don't keep thinking about it. Cindy will be a good distraction. And I'll probably spend the next twenty-four hours half asleep anyway. I'm really tired."

Roman glanced at his watch. "It's getting late. We'll head home, and I'll call in tomorrow to get a status report." He looked Sophia in the eye. "I promise I'll take good care of her, but I want you to be totally at ease with this. If you're not, say so now, and we'll make a different plan."

Sophia glanced at the pleading look in Kylie's eyes and relented. After surviving her kidnapping, her sister certainly had a right to choose her own path to healing, but it did sting a bit that Kylie had chosen a stranger over family. Still, Kylie was a teenager, and Sophia tried to be understanding.

Sophia had been more like a mother to her sister ever since their parents had died a few years ago, and Kylie was at that age when she was trying to spread her wings and figure out who she wanted to be and how she was going to get there.

Had Sophia pushed Kylie away, too, in her quest to avoid being hurt? It was certainly possible. She resolved to work on that relationship, as well, but also to give Kylie space to heal from the trauma in her own way and in her own time. She would make herself available and follow Kylie's lead as they moved forward.

After Roman and Kylie had left, Noah checked his watch and approached Sophia. "It's late. Do you want me to take you to a hotel? I don't think your apartment is safe yet, so I don't think you should go home—not until we find out who is behind the bombing, anyway. But you do need rest. We both do. Another night of sleeping in this conference room isn't going to be good for either of us."

Sophia sat in front of one of the computers, but she didn't start typing. She seemed deep in contemplation, so Noah seated himself, as well, wondering where her thoughts had taken her. He didn't have to wait long.

"Why did you decide to become a policeman, Noah? I never would have guessed you'd end up being a detective."

Noah laughed, taken aback by the sudden twist. He had to admit the question surprised him. "Well, where did you think I would land?"

Sophia shrugged. "I really don't know. You seemed to like a lot of different things back then, but you weren't really serious about any of them."

Noah considered that. "I guess you're right." He decided to answer her question with a question. "How about you? Why did you decide to become an investigative reporter?"

She tilted her head, as if considering.

Finally, she spoke again. "I became a journalist because I wanted to change my corner of the world for the better, and it's important to me to raise awareness about issues that I'm passionate about. Over the last few years, I've discovered that I can make a real difference with my writing. Sometimes, even the smallest article gets read by the right person and can lead to big changes. If I can improve the lives of the people around me, then I'm satisfied."

She aimlessly drew a circle with her finger on the table, then suddenly stopped and met his eye, her expression grim. "I had a friend that got injured when she went horseback riding. It was nobody's fault, but she hurt her back rather badly after being thrown off and became a paraplegic. She also got a rather nasty concussion.

"I started my career by writing a story specifically to educate people about the sport. I didn't want people to stop riding horses, but I did want them to know and understand the dangers, and to take proper safety precautions. Horses are big and powerful, and sometimes they are easily frightened and behave erratically. My friend would still have gone riding, but if she'd been wearing a helmet, her injuries would have been less severe." She shrugged and gave him a playful nudge. "I guess the bottom line is that I want to help people. Okay, your turn."

So, he hadn't deflected her question after all. He sighed. "I don't tell many people this, but I know I can trust you to be discreet." He paused, then pushed forward. "You remember my sister, Candace?"

"Sure. She was like ten years older than you, right? She used to babysit me when I was younger. If I remember correctly, she moved up north to go to college and then got a job in New York City selling real estate, I believe."

"That's right. Well, my freshman year of college, she was working late one night and decided to take the train home to Brooklyn after showing an apartment. She was assaulted and left for dead in an alley."

"Oh, Noah! I'm so sorry!"

"Me, too. It took them over a year to catch the guy, but by that time, he had assaulted three other women. I was just a dumb college kid, but I saw what it did to Candace, and I can imagine what it did to the others. Even now, she's afraid to go out at night and rarely leaves her apartment. She was so vibrant and full of life before it happened. Now she has become a veritable recluse.

"I vowed to become a police officer so I could help other victims. The officers who worked her case treated her well and tried their best to catch the perpetrator. They never gave up. They inspired me and taught me that I could make a difference." He met her eye.

"I'm trying to change my corner of the world for the better, too."

She reached over and squeezed his hand. "Thank you for answering my question. I can tell that's not an easy story to share, but I'm grateful that you told me."

Noah was overwhelmed with the urge to kiss her, right there in the conference room with the window shades wide open and in full view of everyone still left in the bullpen. He glanced toward the windows. There were still a few cops at their desks, but most were done for the day and had already left.

He turned back to Sophia. Her lips seemed so red, sweet and inviting. It was all he could do not to reach out and touch her, to trace the softness with his fingertips. The air felt electrified. But he didn't dare kiss her like he wanted to. Even though they had just shared something personal, he still had no idea how she felt about him. She was grateful, sure. And he could call her a friend again. But was there anything more? It was still too soon to press—too soon to even ask direct questions about her feelings. Still, he had to know if he had even the smallest chance, so he opted for asking a simple question that would leave things open to future possibilities.

"When this is all over, do you think I could take you out to dinner?" He held his breath, hoping she couldn't tell that he was doing so as he waited for an answer.

She paused for a moment, studying his face, then broke out into a smile. "I'd like that," she responded softly.

He exhaled, thankful that he had taken the chance. He didn't know what the future held for either of them, but at least now he had something to look forward to once this entire mess was over and done.

SEVENTEEN

"Who performs blood tests besides doctors?" Sophia asked as they discussed the possibilities out loud. They had spent the night in separate hotel rooms, Noah's adjoining Sophia's, so he could hear her if there was a problem.

They had returned to the conference room at the police station early this morning after a quick breakfast at the hotel. Noah was reusing the teal paisley tie that Sophia liked more and more each time she looked at it. But neither one of them had been prepared for another day away from their apartments, so they had stopped by a department store on their way to the hotel and had done the fastest shopping trip in history to get a few essentials.

Today she wore the same shoes, but she had found a navy pair of slacks and a professional-looking turquoise button-down shirt at a bargain price that she really liked. She'd even found an inexpensive but attractive necklace on the way out of the store that was just enough bling to spice up the outfit without going overboard.

They had decided to dig deeper into Arlo's past, and they were well aware of the time crunch they were facing. The jury was still out deliberating, but could come back at any time. If Arlo Prensky truly was as innocent as his family claimed, Sophia and Noah wanted to prove it before the jury handed down a sentence that would be a serious miscarriage of justice. They also needed to find out who had gassed them at the university and set the bomb at Maggie's apartment.

Noah leaned back in his chair as he took a sip from his coffee cup. "Medical clinics and blood donation sites both handle blood tests."

"And all of that blood has to go to a lab somewhere. How hard would it be for someone to get their hands on a vial or two of Prensky's blood?"

"Labs have security, and they have to follow strict federal guidelines. Plus, if what you're suggesting is true, that would mean that Maggie Spencer's death was premeditated and not a crime of opportunity, like we've been thinking."

Noah suddenly pulled the laptop closer, put his coffee cup down and started typing. It was clear that something vital had just occurred to him.

"What is it?"

"Remember that study I said Prensky was participating in at the university?"

"Sure. You said it was some sort of medication trial."

"Right. Well, what if they did blood draws as part of their study?"

Sophia snapped her fingers. "Excellent idea. And that sort of lab might have less security than a hospital."

Noah nodded, got a number from the report he had pulled up and dialed the researcher he had originally interviewed about the study. After a ten-minute conversation, he made another quick call, then put the phone down. He turned to Sophia, who was waiting anxiously to hear what he had discovered.

"The study Arlo participated in was related to diabetes. It required frequent medical checkups and blood draws associated with a blind study of a medication they were testing for the medical school." He leaned closer.

"The lab they used for the blood work was part of the university hospital system. It's located on the second floor of the medical school." He grinned. "The lab had a break-in the day before Maggie's murder, but they didn't notice much missing other than a few vials of blood. They wanted to keep the theft low-key because they were worried their study would be shut down if the school discovered the vials had been stolen." He raised an eyebrow. "Although they claimed they reported it, *somehow* the report never got filed with the university police."

"Somehow?" Sophia scoffed. Still, she could sense Noah's excitement. It was contagious. "Was Prensky's blood the only blood that was taken?"

"No. Three other students had to come in and give a second donation, but they didn't complain because they got paid extra for their time. Since Prensky was out of the study anyway because of his arrest, the study staff didn't worry about his missing blood."

"Who knew Prensky was part of the study?" Sophia asked.

"They're sending me over a list now of everyone who was aware of the participants. It's a small list, but they're being rather cooperative because they're worried about the theft coming to light. They're also sending over some of the basic information about the study, like the protocols, the participant survey and other details that they're allowed to share with the general public. It's all basic information, but we might see something pop.

"My second call just now was to Roman. He's getting a search warrant as we speak to find out who had access to the lab where the blood was stored. You have to have a keycard to bypass the security system, so if we can get the university's security records, we should see everyone that entered and left the lab that day."

Sophia's brow creased. "But wouldn't they have already checked that log when they discovered the missing blood?"

"Yes, but there weren't any red flags. There was no forced entry into the lab. The lab tech I talked to tried to convince me that someone had just broken a few vials in error or labeled them incorrectly. He really tried to downplay the entire incident and didn't even want to admit that any blood was missing, despite what the records show. I think he's really scared that he will get blamed and it will cost him his job. Also, there aren't any security cameras in the lab to prove the blood was actually stolen. Since they didn't want to accuse anyone without proof, they just quietly got the second blood draws from the students and went on with business as usual."

Sophia jumped up and started pacing. "We're so close, I can feel it." She stopped for a moment and regarded Noah closely. "Do you think Angie Carmichael had access to the lab? That woman's attitude still bothers me."

Noah nodded. "It's certainly possible. She was never a person of interest before, but now I'm starting to wonder." He took out a fresh pack of Doublemint gum and offered one to Sophia before grabbing one for himself. She refused but gave him a smile.

Noah picked up his phone and made another quick call, then reported his findings. "That was the state attorney's office. The jury is still out. She says this is normal, and sometimes it takes a jury three or four days to deliberate and come up with a verdict. She said she'd call as soon as she hears anything."

He tapped something on his computer, and his email jumped onto the page. "Okay, here's the information about the study and the list of people who had access to the participants' names."

Sophia came to read the screen over his shoulder. There were four names of professors who were managing the drug study and four graduate student names. It was hard to keep the disappointment from her voice. "Angie isn't on it. I guess she wouldn't be. She's a chemistry grad student, not a doctor or a premed student working on the drug trial." She leaned closer. "Do you recognize any of the names?"

"No." Noah hit a few more keys, his frustration evident. "Wait—here's another email." He opened this one, and they both read the names of the study's consultants. The email contained three additional names of people to be contacted if questions arose that related to their fields of expertise.

"'Professor Reginald Keenan,'" they simultaneously read out loud.

"Oh, wow," Sophia said, surprised yet pleased at the same time. "You'd better call Roman back. Now we need a subpoena for Keenan's computer, too."

Noah nodded. "I was just thinking the same thing. I bet this all boils down to that academic paper Keenan got published. The one that Maggie Spencer wrote. He needed the credit to keep his job, and he killed her to keep it quiet."

"It certainly gives Keenan motive," Sophia agreed. "But why would Keenan frame Arlo? I mean, why pick that guy?"

"I have no idea," Noah mused. "We never found any connection between the two. If they had met before, we certainly found no record of it," he said tightly. He called Roman and asked for the additional warrant. While they were waiting, he downloaded and printed two copies of the medication study overview and all of the attachments, then gave one copy to Sophia and kept one for himself. "Let's look these over while we wait for the warrants."

"What are we looking for?"

"I have no idea. I hope we'll know it when we see it," he said as he handed her the papers.

Sophia started reading. They were making good progress. She fervently hoped they would be able to discover the truth before Arlo Prensky's jury returned with a verdict.

Noah set aside the fifty-two-page overview of the study and rubbed his eyes. He wasn't even sure he understood everything he had just read since most of it had been written by doctors, for doctors, but he hadn't seen anything in the report that would tie Keenan to Prensky. He turned to the attachments, then glanced over at Sophia, hoping that she'd been able to absorb and analyze what they were reading better than he had.

"Anything?" she asked.

"Not yet. You?"

"This stuff is drier than wallpaper paste. I think I'd actually rather watch golf on TV than read another one of these studies."

Noah smiled. "Even the Masters?" he quipped, mentioning the illustrious golf tournament played in Georgia once a year in April.

"Yes, even the Masters," she agreed. "Could anything be more boring?"

Noah laughed and returned to his reading. The first two attachments, graphs of the chemical components included in the study, meant nothing to him. But the third attachment was much more interesting. It was the survey completed by all prospective participants to determine their suitability for the study.

"Check this out," Noah said as soon as he had read the survey in its entirety. "A lot of these questions are asking for a psychological profile of the applicant. I'm no expert, but they go a lot further than just trying to decipher a person's medical history."

Sophia flipped to the survey and started reading the questions. "You're right. It looks like they wanted to make sure the person was at least stable enough to stick with the study. They also probably wanted to verify that the participant wasn't taking any psychotropic medication or other drugs that would be contraindicated for the medication they were testing."

"Keenan was a consultant. According to the introductory documents, he would have had full access to the completed surveys..." Noah started to say.

"Which means he would have known that Prensky had a family, but didn't have a steady job or other means of support." Sophia finished the thought.

"With just a little bit of research, Keenan could have discovered all he needed to know about Arlo Prensky. We may never know exactly why he chose him over the others, but something in this survey must have made Keenan feel like Prensky would be a good person to frame for the murder. Then it was just a matter of stealing the vials, killing

Maggie and staging the scene with Arlo's blood," Noah said fervently.

"Do you think Keenan kept the older versions of the article on his computer? We'd need those to prove his motive, right?"

"We have the draft that we got at Maggie's apartment, but even if we find some of the older versions, I still think we need more. Hopefully, when we seize Keenan's computer, we can also find some old emails or other proof that will bolster our theory. If they aren't on his computer, we might be able to subpoena the university's server to see if they have any of the older emails. We'll just take it one step at a time."

The door to the conference room suddenly opened and Charlie came striding in. He gave them both a nod, and Noah rose to greet him. "Welcome back to the big city! How'd you like Flint Rock?" The two men shook hands, and Charlie clapped Noah on the back with a good-natured grin.

"It's a hole-in-the-wall compared to Atlanta. If you blink twice, you'll miss it when you drive through, but it's a nice enough little town," Charlie answered.

Noah laughed, knowing that his partner had been raised in Atlanta and preferred the larger metropolis over the smaller towns any day. He turned and reintroduced him to Sophia. She thanked him profusely for his help with finding her sister, and finally Charlie handed some papers over to Noah.

"I almost forgot about these. Roman asked me to give them to you. He said he knows a guy over at the Atlanta University police force, and was able to expedite the warrant for the passcode information at the hospital laboratory. One of these documents is the list of people who had access to the lab during the time frame that you were interested in."

Noah quickly perused the sheets and found what he was looking for. He read through the names, then looked up and met Sophia's eyes. "Reginald Keenan was the last person to access the lab the night before Maggie's murder." He flipped a page. "And here's an affidavit saying the door is intact, has never required service and shows no signs of tampering or forced entry."

"That's a smoking gun if I've ever seen one," Sophia replied, her eyes bright.

Noah looked back over at Charlie. "Did Roman say whether or not he'd gotten the subpoena for Keenan's computer?"

"He said it was on its way and you'll have

it in thirty minutes or less. He actually requested two. One for Keenan's computer at his office at the university and one for his home computer and laptop. He said his friend at the university is on standby and will execute the warrant as soon as it comes through."

Noah smiled and rubbed his hands together. "I love it when a plan comes together. Want to execute a search with us at Professor Keenan's home?" He quickly recapped everything they had learned in the last few hours to bring Charlie up to speed on their working theory. "Now we know Keenan had access to Prensky's blood. All we need now is proof of his motive, and we'll be ready to make the arrest."

"I'd be delighted to join you," Charlie answered, once he had a clear understanding of what was happening. He took a sip from the coffee cup he had brought in with him and then tossed it in the trash and grimaced.

"Wow, that's awful. Did you make the coffee again, Noah?"

"Wasn't me," Noah said, his hands raised. "Blame Matthews for that brew. I couldn't swallow it, either. Thankfully, I got a cup of the good stuff at the hotel this morning."

Charlie laughed as the three left the conference room and headed to the parking deck to get their car for the drive to Keenan's house. Charlie kept in contact with Roman while Noah drove, making sure they would know the instant the search warrant was signed and electronically delivered to the officer's phone. Sophia rode along and had agreed to stay in the car while the officers were performing the search.

Noah felt conflicted as he drove. He had been so sure Arlo Prensky was guilty. A sinking feeling started churning in his gut.

Had he arrested the wrong man?

EIGHTEEN

"Police! Open up!" Noah shouted. He banged on the door, then moved out of the way so one of the uniformed officers who had joined them could breach the door and break the lock. It only took one strong blow to force the door open. The officer moved back and out of the way as the door swung worthlessly from its hinges and fell back against the door frame. Noah and Charlie entered, their weapons drawn.

They moved silently through the house, looking for their quarry, but they heard nothing as they searched the kitchen, living room and dining room. The other officer searched the bedrooms in the back of the house and returned moments later, holstering his weapon. The house appeared empty.

"The back rooms are clear," the officer reported.

Just then, they heard a noise from the rear yard. The three officers rushed to the back door and noticed Professor Keenan just as he finished pouring lighter fluid over some dark items in an outdoor decorative firepit. He had a lighter in his right hand, an empty lighter fluid can in his left.

"Light that, Professor Keenan, and it will be the last thing you ever do," Noah threatened as he approached the older man, his gun pointing at the professor's midriff. The acrid odor of the lighter fluid permeated his nostrils.

"Hands up!" Charlie ordered, close behind Noah. The other officer had also drawn his weapon again and was also pointing it at the professor.

"Don't shoot!" Keenan pleaded, clearly surprised by the officers' arrival. Dropping the lighter and the can of lighter fluid, he took a step back.

Noah and his team kept advancing until Noah was right behind Keenan. He holstered his weapon and pulled out his handcuffs. "Having a barbecue?" he asked lightly as he cuffed the man's right hand and pulled it behind him, tugging back his other arm to do the same.

Charlie scrunched his nose and held up a laptop that he pulled from the firepit with two fingers. The lighter fluid dripped from the casing and landed in a pool at the bottom of the pit. "I prefer ribs or maybe a good steak."

"Reginald Keenan, you have the right to remain silent..." Noah recited the rest of the Miranda warnings. "Do you understand these rights as I have explained them to you?"

Once he finished with Keenan, he handed him over to the officer to watch while he sifted through the pile of computer equipment that filled the firepit. If they had arrived even five minutes later, they would have probably lost all of this evidence. Noah was no computer expert, but he imagined it would have been hard to recover all of the data stored on the various pieces of equipment if they had been destroyed by fire.

Noah pushed aside the laptop and noticed a desktop computer and a computer bag. He pulled out the bag and found another laptop, as well as two hard drives secured inside.

Keenan raised his chin. "I did not murder that woman," he insisted. "She was trying to destroy me, but I didn't kill her."

"If that's true, then I'm wondering why you have her laptop and hard drives here and were about to cook them for dinner. According to all reports, Maggie Spencer had them with her when she died."

Keenan looked away, but Noah smiled. He would interview the man again once Roman and the lab techs had a chance to find out exactly what was on all of these computers. Whether the man confessed or not, Noah was confident they had just found enough evidence to prove his motive. "No worries, Professor. I would like to know how you learned how to make a bomb, though, and also how you gassed us in the basement at the university."

"Any decent chemistry student can make a bomb," Keenan sneered. It was a tacit admission regarding the gas incident, and Noah pushed forward with another question.

"So your plan was to make sure we stopped reinvestigating the murder by killing us?"

"It would have looked like an accident," he said under his breath.

Noah raised his eyebrow, surprised the professor had just acknowledged that, especially with Charlie and the other officer there to verify the admission. He couldn't wait to share the news with Sophia, who was still waiting in their car.

The man's shoulders sagged, and he suddenly lost his haughty demeanor as he realized what he had just done.

"Why couldn't you leave well enough alone? Prensky is a loser. He'll never amount to anything. He deserves to go to prison. Have you seen his rap sheet?" Keenan's lip curled. "Only a handful of people understand perovskite instability, and I am one of them. That little grad student thought she knew more than me about the subject. She was going to destroy everything that I'd achieved, including my reputation. I couldn't let her get away with it."

"So you destroyed *her* reputation instead? Took away *her* chances at a future in chemistry to feed your ego?" Noah took a step forward. "Then you took *her life*?"

The professor straightened his spine and narrowed his eyes. "There are hundreds of chemistry grad students in the world, Detective." He looked Noah up and down. "Just like there are hundreds of detectives crawling the earth. I've been in this field for thirty years. I've seen grad students come and go. I am the expert everyone turns to and calls when they want a reference or an opinion. I am the one who deserves the notoriety. Not that upstart nobody Maggie Spencer."

"What about Joanna, Maggie's roommate? Did she deserve to die, too?" Noah asked.

Keenan actually looked surprised. "I didn't bomb Maggie's apartment. I swear I didn't."

"We'll see," Noah said quietly. He'd heard enough. Right now, he had to get to the courthouse before there was a serious miscarriage of justice. He left Keenan with Charlie and the other officer, who was calling in the arrest and asking for the crime scene team to come and collect the evidence.

Sophia ran up the courthouse steps behind Noah, hoping that they arrived in time. It wasn't an easy thing to get a person released once a conviction was handed down by the jury, and Sophia didn't want Arlo Prensky to spend one more hour in jail than he already had.

Noah had been unable to reach the prosecutor because, according to her assistant, she was in court on another matter, but that same assistant had also just called them to announce that the attorney would soon be in the courtroom since Arlo's jury had returned and court was again in session.

Noah burst through the courtroom doors with Sophia on his heels. Normally, he would have met with the prosecutor alone before the hearing to discuss what they had discovered. Law enforcement and the prosecutor's office were on the same team, and they worked together to gain a conviction. Today, though, there simply wasn't time. "Stop the proceedings!" he announced, causing all eyes in the courtroom to turn to them.

The judge banged his gavel to quiet the room. "What's the meaning of this interruption, Detective?" he demanded.

"I have just uncovered new evidence that is vital to this case. I must speak to Your Honor and counsel in chambers."

The judge frowned. "This is highly irregular."

"I understand that, and I do apologize. Please indulge me, Your Honor. I promise you won't be disappointed. If I can just have a five-minute recess, I will be able to explain everything."

The prosecutor glared at Noah. Once the judge acquiesced and stood, the bailiff yelled "All rise" over the cacophony as the judge left the courtroom, clearly expecting the rest of them to follow.

The prosecutor waved Noah over as she slowly followed the judge and the defense attorney. "What's this about, Detective?"

"We've got the wrong man," Noah said tightly for the prosecutor's ears alone. He wanted the lawyer to have at least a short heads-up before they went into the judge's office. "We need to fix this now before it goes any further."

The prosecutor's face turned scarlet red, but she followed Noah toward the door leading out of the courtroom and to the judge's office, which was just a few steps down the hallway.

"Law enforcement and court staff personnel only," the bailiff announced as Sophia tried to follow the group inside.

"She's with me," Noah said stiffly, meeting the bailiff's eye. "She needs to be in there, too, in case the judge has any questions that I can't answer and she can."

The bailiff paused a moment but finally shrugged. "As long as you're vouching for her. The judge still might throw her out, though."

"We'll take that chance," Sophia said as she stiffened her spine. She had come this far, and she wanted to see it through.

The judge was obviously still not pleased about having the case interrupted, and he made that clear as soon as everyone had entered his office. "Okay," he said loudly as the door closed behind the last of the group. "Get on with your explanation, Detective, and do it quickly."

"I'm sorry to barge in so dramatically," Noah said evenly, "but I needed to talk to you immediately before the jury returned and convicted an innocent man."

"Aha!" the defense attorney said with a smile.

"Hush, and let the man talk," the judge admonished. He turned back to Noah. "Go ahead."

"I tried to contact the state attorney, Your Honor, but she was unavailable, and so I had no choice but to come directly to your courtroom. As you know, I was the arresting officer in this case, but new evidence has just come to light." He motioned toward Sophia. "This is Sophia Archer. With her help, we were able to reopen the Spencer investigation as certain facts came to light that were pertinent to a different case.

"To make a long story short, we just arrested Reginald Keenan, a professor at Atlanta State University. During the arrest, Keenan uttered several statements that made it clear he was responsible for Maggie Spencer's murder. I believe those statements, along with the evidence we seized at the university and at Keenan's home, will show that he was the real murderer, not Arlo Prensky—"

"I expect a full dismissal," the defense attorney demanded suddenly, interrupting Noah as he pushed toward the judge's desk. "This is unbelievable."

"Hold on," the judge said as he put up his hand. He turned to the prosecutor. "How do you want to proceed?"

"Obviously, we'll need time to take a look at this new evidence and to consider the statements. I ask that the court grant us a continuance of twenty-four hours so we can see exactly what the detective and Ms. Archer have uncovered. If it all pans out as Detective Bradley suggests, then at the end of that period, the state will dismiss the charges against Mr. Prensky and file new charges against Reginald Keenan."

"Mr. Prensky should be released immediately, and the charges should be dropped right this minute," the defense attorney demanded petulantly.

"Motion denied," the judge said firmly. "Prensky has waited this long. He can wait another twenty-four hours to make sure the state attorney has her ducks in a row." He looked at the prosecutor again. "You've got your twenty-four hours. I'll release the jury and bring them back tomorrow. By then, you'd better have a plan of action mapped out in this case. Got it?"

"Yes, sir," the state attorney replied crisply.

The group filed out, and the prosecutor pulled Noah and Sophia to the side. "Are you two sure about this?"

Noah nodded. "I wouldn't have interrupted the court proceedings otherwise. Our crime scene investigation team is at the professor's house right now, seizing the computers and items we need to prove motive. Two other officers heard Keenan's statements after I Mirandized him."

The state attorney nodded. "Okay. Send me everything you have by the end of the day. That should give you enough time to verify his statements and tie this all together." She rubbed her forehead absently as if she had a headache forming behind her eyes.

"I'm sorry about the late notice," Noah offered. "I promise we acted as soon as we discovered the new evidence."

"I trust you, Detective," she replied. "But I'm glad you got here when you did. I'd rather know that we got it wrong now than learn the truth after the jury published the verdict." She looked at Sophia and gave her a weary smile. "I was glad to hear your sister was found safe and sound. I'm sorry you and your family got dragged into this mess."

"Thank you. I appreciate that," Sophia responded, meaning it.

"Any idea which way the jury was leaning?" Noah asked.

"According to the bailiff, they were going to vote guilty."

NINETEEN

Sophia moved toward the door to her apartment, surprised by the knock. She glanced through the peephole, then smiled and opened the door.

"Detective."

"Miss Archer. May I come in?" He showed her a bag from the local Italian restaurant and opened it slightly so she could see the contents.

"A man bearing dinner. My favorite kind of visitor," Sophia quipped. She opened the door wider so he could enter and then followed him into her dining room, where he immediately began unpacking the bag.

"I hope you don't have too many men showing up at your door with dinner," he said in response. He raised an eyebrow at her, and she grinned and laughed unrepentantly.

"It's a rare thing, I assure you."

Noah smiled. "I wasn't sure what you liked, so I brought a little bit of everything."

"I'll say," she agreed as she helped unpack and read the labels on the containers. "Eggplant Parmesan, lasagna with meat sauce, fettuccine Alfredo with chicken…" She took out the bread. "There's enough here to feed an army."

"Well, I was hoping you were hungry. You didn't eat much during the investigation, so I wanted to make sure you got a good meal."

He pushed the bag aside and took a small step toward her, then another. Their eyes locked as he stopped directly in front of her, and the air sizzled and sparked with the current suddenly flowing between them. A shy smile slid across his face as he reached up and slowly drew his finger down her cheek. His finger moved to her lips and lightly traced them back and forth. Then he gently pulled her into his arms and kissed her fervently. She was dazed at first, but then responded in kind as electricity shot from her lips clear down to her toes. He finally stopped and pulled back, and she laughed in response.

"What was that for?" she asked as she touched her lips with her fingertips.

"I've been wanting to do that all week," he

said with a hesitant smile. "You kissed me back. Does that mean…?"

"It means it's my turn." This time she gently pulled his head down and initiated the kiss herself. It was a sweet kiss, full of promise. "Thank you for dinner."

"Wow," he answered with a grin. "If that's how you respond when I bring dinner over, I'll have to do this a lot more often."

Sophia drew her knuckles down the side of his face in a sweet caress, then stepped back. "Sounds like a plan."

Noah took the rest of the items out of the bag while Sophia got plates, utensils and a few serving spoons and brought them to the table.

They said grace, then sat together to enjoy the meal.

"Can you tell me where things stand with the Keenan case?" Sophia asked after she tried a bit of eggplant. She suddenly rolled her eyes and grinned. "Oh, my gosh. This is delicious."

Noah grinned back and served himself a healthy portion of fettuccine Alfredo. "I also know the best Chinese place in town. If you're game, we can try that one next."

"I'm game," she said with a wink. "But

you'll have to promise to give my favorite Greek restaurant a try in return. The chef makes an amazing gyro, and the salad that goes with it is sublime."

"Deal."

Sophia watched Noah as he took a bite and savored the food. She felt her heart beat even more rapidly as she remembered the kisses they had just shared. The first one had surprised her, but she had liked it so much she had come back for more.

It had been two days since they had interrupted the courtroom to inform the judge of Keenan's confession, and Noah had been so tied up with work that he hadn't been able to do much besides call her once a day to check on her. The time apart had been short, but it had solidified some of the feelings that she had been sorting through ever since Keenan had been arrested.

The past was over and done. The Noah she knew now was an intriguing mixture of the boy she had known and the caring and professional man he had become. The man she had discovered during the investigation. As they had worked closely together, Sophia had seen a side of Noah that she'd never seen before— the serious law enforcement officer who was committed to justice. The detective who had rushed to make sure an innocent man wasn't wrongly convicted. The caring and considerate man who had stood by her side and helped her through the horrible stress she had experienced when her sister was kidnapped.

In Sophia's book, the man she had seen emerge was definitely worth getting to know better. If Noah was amenable, and he certainly seemed to be, then she was all in and ready to see where this relationship could go.

"So, how is Kylie doing?" Noah asked as he took a slice of bread and buttered it.

"She's doing great. She is a poster child for resiliency. We spent the day together, but she wanted to go back over to Roman's to spend the night one last time before she heads back to Flint Rock tomorrow morning." Sophia took a piece of bread for herself. "She has really bonded with Cindy, and I think she even talked Roman's sister into going to Flint Rock University in the fall."

"That's great to hear, and Roman will be grateful that she encouraged Cindy to go to college. He's had his hands full with her. You may think he was helping you by taking Kylie, but I think it was actually the other way around." He took her hand and squeezed it gently, then released it again. "Time will heal a lot of her wounds, and with your support, I'm sure she'll be okay. I'm so glad we found her when we did."

She rewarded him with another smile. She just couldn't seem to stop smiling. "So what's new with the Keenan case?"

"A lot," Noah said as he added a helping of lasagna to his plate. "Roman and the computer team were able to access both Keenan's desktop and his laptop, as well as Maggie's laptop. They also got a host of old email conversations from the university servers that Keenan thought he had deleted. Altogether, they recovered ample proof that Keenan stole Maggie's research and plagiarized her article. I've been in communication with the journal, and they'll be reprinting it, giving Maggie credit for the work. It's a huge embarrassment for the university—not to mention the publicity nightmare of having one of their top professors tried for the murder of a grad student."

"Is there going to be a trial?"

"There is now. Keenan says he never actually confessed to the murder, and once I went back over our conversation a few times in my head, I realized he was right. He sure was glad she was dead, and her laptop was recovered at his house, but he never actually confessed to killing her. Even so, his statements were very incriminating. With all of the circumstantial evidence that we discovered, I don't think the state attorney will have too much trouble convincing a jury."

"I agree. Keenan is crazy if he doesn't accept a plea bargain, but he's so prideful that he might end up doing the maximum, just because he's too stubborn to deal."

Noah took a drink from his water glass. "Keenan did admit to locking us in the basement at the university and trying to kill us with the gas, so he's facing a minimum of two attempted murder charges on top of everything else. One way or another, he's going to prison for a very long time. The only thing we haven't been able to pin down is the bombing at Maggie's apartment building. Keenan is maintaining his innocence."

"What about Arlo Prensky?" Sophia asked.

"His case was dismissed. He was released yesterday. I went to see John Prensky at the jail to let him know, and I apologized to him and his family. It was a hard thing to do, but it was the right thing. I told him I'd testify at his trial about my mistake, too, as long as you were okay with that."

Sophia considered it for a moment, then nodded. "Yes, I think that's the right thing to do."

The doorbell rang and Noah quirked his brow. "Are you expecting someone?"

"No. I have no idea who it could be." She wiped her hands on a napkin and went to the door. "Actually, is it Girl Scout cookie time yet? I have two that live in the building, and I've promised them both a sale. Maybe it's one of them with a box of thin mints or samoas."

Sophia opened the door, still facing Noah, then screamed as Angie pushed her way inside and grabbed Sophia from behind, a sharp knife at her throat.

"You ruined everything," Angie said vehemently. "And now you're going to pay."

Noah stood slowly, keeping his hands wide apart so his movements wouldn't scare Angie and force the knife into Sophia's throat. A tiny line of blood was already visible where the knife was biting into her skin. "Whoa now, Ms. Carmichael. Hold on there. If you're upset with someone, it should be Professor Keenan. He's the one who killed Maggie Spencer."

"You think so?" Angie said, her tone bitter. "Keenan thinks he walks on water, but the truth is, he would be nothing without me. I'm the one who put that cell phone jammer in Maggie's office, and I'm the one that took his ID card and got Prensky's blood from the lab. I was the one who planned the whole thing. He couldn't have gotten rid of Maggie without me. He promised me her position and that he would make my career if I helped him. And now what do I have? Nothing but a tarnished reputation, all because of this woman's interference. Now she's going to pay!"

Angie's eyes were wide, and it was clear that she was not in control of her actions. Noah swallowed as trepidation filled him. He couldn't lose Sophia. He would be completely lost without her in his life. He knew that now, without a doubt. He met Sophia's eyes and tried to calm the fear he saw amplifying there. His mind spun as he struggled to figure out a way to reach Angie and to get the knife away from Sophia's throat at the same time.

Suddenly an idea came to him and he took a step forward, then another. When he spoke, his voice was calm and soothing.

"Ms. Carmichael, I can help you, but we

need Sophia. She's a writer. Well, actually, she's a reporter for the *Atlanta Times*. Her articles reach thousands of people, and she can tell your story." He took another step. "People are going to hear about Keenan and what he did, and they're going to wonder who was the force behind him. They're going to want to know about you and everything you did to help. Sophia can make that happen."

He was only about six feet away now and could see that the woman was considering his words. "Are you sure she can do that?"

"I'm positive," Noah answered. "She just won an award for her writing last month. She's well-known and can reach the masses." He tried even harder to make his voice sound enthusiastic while also as gentle and comforting as possible. "She's your best hope at getting the respect you deserve, Ms. Carmichael. You don't want to hurt her. Why don't you put that knife down and have some dinner with us? We can talk about it right here and now." He took another step and kept his eyes sweeping between Angie Carmichael's face and the knife she was holding.

"Do you like Italian?" he asked softly. "The lasagna is excellent. I'm sure you'll want to give it a try."

The next few seconds went by in a blur. Angie lowered the knife about an inch from Sophia's neck, but then her muscles suddenly tightened in her arm and Noah could actually see from her body language the exact moment when she decided to kill Sophia.

He wasn't going to let that happen.

Smooth as silk, he pulled his personal 9 mm out of the holster he wore at his back and fired, hitting Angie and killing her instantly. The knife fell to the floor, clattering when it hit the tile just seconds before Angie's body collapsed.

"Noah…" Sophia said faintly, holding out her arms. She seemed afraid to move, but Noah didn't wait for another invitation. He pulled her into his embrace and away from Angie's body.

"You're safe," he crooned. "She'll never hurt you again."

Sophia was shaking from head to toe, and Noah quickly led her to the living room and sat with her on the couch. He pulled her into his arms again, comforting her.

"I can't believe she instigated Maggie's murder."

Noah brushed a lock of Sophia's hair back

behind her ear. "I can't, either. I didn't see that one coming."

"Neither did I. I bet she was even the one in that white sedan that was following us after Keenan's arrest."

"You're probably right."

Noah gently cupped Sophia's face with his hands and traced his fingers slowly along her eyebrows, her cheeks and chin. With a delicate touch, he moved to her neck and inspected where Angie had pressed the knife against Sophia's skin. "You have a small cut here, and it's bleeding a little, but I don't think you'll need stitches. Still, I'll take you to the hospital if you want to go. It's up to you."

Sophia shook her head. "No, thank you. I'll be okay." She squeezed his hand. "I know you have to call and report this. Just hold me for a minute or two more before you do. That's all I ask."

"Absolutely. There's no place else I'd rather be."

EPILOGUE

"And now I'd like to introduce the winner of the Pembroke Prize for Outstanding Journalism, the highest honor short of winning the Pulitzer that a journalist can receive. Miss Sophia Archer."

Sophia smiled as she stood. As the room erupted into loud applause, she nodded graciously and headed toward the stage. She wasn't sure she agreed with the characterization of the award she had just won—there were several good awards out there for excellence in journalism—but she wasn't one to quibble, and she was very humbled that they had chosen her as the recipient.

She made it to the stage without incident, pleased that she hadn't tripped or somehow embarrassed herself on the way, and took the award from the MC who left her with the trophy at the podium. She waited for the audience to stop clapping and take their seats again, gazing back and forth at the two hundred or so people who had come to the award dinner.

"Before I start my very short speech, let me first say thank you to Noah Bradley, one of Atlanta's finest detectives. Without him, I wouldn't be able to stand before you today. Detective Bradley saved my life and the life of my sister. He is my strength, and I love him unconditionally."

More applause erupted, and she motioned for Noah to stand. He did so reluctantly, and he didn't appear pleased with the attention. Nonetheless, he nodded and waved to the crowd and quickly took his seat again.

When his gaze returned to hers, she was overwhelmed by the love she saw shining in his eyes. He completed her. It seemed corny to think that, but she, a famous wordsmith and writer, could really not describe it any better. The last six months of her life had been a whirlwind; she had gotten to know Noah all over again as they'd dated and grown in their relationship. He had even started attending her church and was now teaching a men's class there on Thursday evenings. She had seen enormous growth in her own life due to his encouragement, and their relationship was even stronger now that Christ was at the center.

She couldn't remember being happier.

She finished her speech and returned to her chair among a standing ovation. The MC returned to the stage and invited the guests to the dance floor to complete the evening's agenda.

Noah gave her a quick kiss as she returned to her seat and studied the trophy she had just won. It was a blue-crystal bird flying toward the sky attached to an attractive marble stand where her name, the name of the award and the date were engraved in a large flowing font. It was a classy, artistically crafted award that would look great on her mantel. And it was also a wonderful honor. He met her eye and smiled. "You're amazing, you know that?"

Sophia shrugged. "Awards come and go. It's a wonderful honor, but it's nothing like having you by my side. I meant what I said before I started my speech. I love you, Noah Bradley."

Noah beamed, pleased by her words. "I love you right back, Sophia Archer."

Several colleagues and community leaders suddenly approached, and Sophia stood and shook hands with the people who had come to congratulate her. Finally, after about twenty minutes or so, she turned back to Noah as the crowd thinned. "Ready to go?"

"Go?" he said. "I hear they have a live band tonight. Don't you want to dance?"

"I thought dancing wasn't your thing."

Noah shrugged. "I never said I didn't like it. I just said I wasn't very good at it."

"Ah. In that case, I would love to dance, but only if you feel comfortable doing so."

"Lead the way, princess. I'll follow you anywhere."

She took his hand and led him toward the dance floor, and love swelled within him as he looked at her. The depth of feeling he had for Sophia was not based upon the past. It was a more mature attraction and an even deeper connection than he had ever experienced, all grounded in the people they had become as they had both grown and matured. They had been dating for six months now, ever since Kylie had been rescued, and their relationship was stronger and more vibrant than ever.

He followed her past the buffet tables and, when she stopped near a group of guests also moving to the dance floor, glanced at her shiny patent-leather pumps with the small black bows. "What if I step on your feet?" he whispered for her ears alone.

Sophia laughed. "I'll be sure to move my toes."

He slid his right hand behind her back and grasped her other hand with his left, reveling at the softness of her skin. "Is this where my hands go?" He hesitated, waiting for her correction.

"Perfect!" she said with a smile, making no adjustment.

Noah made eye contact with the band's conductor and gave a small, imperceptible nod. The man nodded in return, raised his baton, and the music began with a flourish of violins.

Noah tilted his head as he listened for a moment. "That sounds like a waltz…"

"Good ear!" Sophia observed. "Look, if you're too uncomfortable…"

Without another word, he swept her out onto the dance floor. On the beat, he led her effortlessly by taking a step forward as she took a step back and started the pattern. She raised an eyebrow as he continued to waltz her down the floor and turn her perfectly in time to the music. Her expression was filled with surprise. "You were teasing me. You've done this before!"

He pulled her back into his arms from the turn. "I might have taken a few lessons…"

She laughed. "Beast! When did you ever have time?"

"A few of us have been going to lessons on Thursday nights after Bible study. They were just a half an hour at a time, but it's amazing how much a person can learn when they are properly motivated."

"And you were motivated?"

He smiled sheepishly. "I wanted to impress you. Did I succeed?"

"Oh, yes," she agreed. It was clear from her expression that she was enjoying herself and the fact that Noah was keeping time, was holding his frame, and had made the effort to learn the steps. He continued to waltz her around the dance floor for the entirety of the song, and he delighted in the feel of her in his arms and the smile that played on her lips. They let the music flow through them, making two into one, and he relished the closeness they were sharing.

As the song ended, the MC who had announced Sophia's award appeared beside them and handed Noah a microphone. He smiled and thanked the man before he stepped away.

Then, checking to be sure the mic's green light was on, Noah turned to Sophia, who had a question in her eye.

"What's going on?" she whispered.

"Sophia Archer, I can't imagine sharing my life with anybody else. You are my light, my sunshine, and you honor me by being by my side."

The crowd thinned around them to form a circle as someone aimed a spotlight on the two of them and lowered the house lights.

Noah bent down on one knee.

Sophia started shaking, and Noah thought he saw tears forming in her eyes as he pulled the ring box out of his pocket, opened it and continued.

"When we were young, I made a list of all of the qualities I wanted to find in a wife, and little did I know, I was describing you the entire time. The way you look at me makes me feel strong and confident, like I can conquer the world, as long as you are by my side. Will you please marry me?"

By now, the tears were really flowing. Sophia pulled him to his feet and embraced him wholeheartedly. "Yes, Noah. I would be hon-ored to marry you."

Noah felt his own eyes start to water as he pulled back for a moment to slip the ring on her finger. "She said yes," he said in the microphone before handing it back to the MC. On cue, the conductor started the music again and Noah leaned forward to softly ask, "Ready for another turn around the dance floor?"

Sophia nodded with tears in her eyes, and the two swept back into the music to a rous-ing round of applause.

Noah said a prayer of thanksgiving, trust-ing God to be with them as they began this journey together and entered the next chapter of their lives as one.

* * * * *

Get 4 FREE REWARDS!

We'll send you 2 FREE Books plus 2 FREE Mystery Gifts.

Love Inspired books feature uplifting stories where faith helps guide you through life's challenges and discover the promise of a new beginning.

FREE
Value Over
$20

YES! Please send me 2 FREE Love Inspired Romance novels and my 2 FREE mystery gifts (gifts are worth about $10 retail). After receiving them, if I don't wish to receive any more books, I can return the shipping statement marked "cancel." If I don't cancel, I will receive 6 brand-new novels every month and be billed just $5.24 each for the regular-print edition or $5.99 each for the larger-print edition in the U.S., or $5.74 each for the regular-print edition or $6.24 each for the larger-print edition in Canada. That's a savings of at least 13% off the cover price. It's quite a bargain! Shipping and handling is just 50¢ per book in the U.S. and $1.25 per book in Canada.* I understand that accepting the 2 free books and gifts places me under no obligation to buy anything. I can always return a shipment and cancel at any time. The free books and gifts are mine to keep no matter what I decide.

Choose one: ☐ Love Inspired Romance
Regular-Print
(105/305 IDN GNWC)

☐ Love Inspired Romance
Larger-Print
(122/322 IDN GNWC)

Name (please print)

Address   Apt. #

City   State/Province   Zip/Postal Code

Email: Please check this box ☐ if you would like to receive newsletters and promotional emails from Harlequin Enterprises ULC and its affiliates. You can unsubscribe anytime.

Mail to the **Harlequin Reader Service:**
IN U.S.A.: P.O. Box 1341, Buffalo, NY 14240-8531
IN CANADA: P.O. Box 603, Fort Erie, Ontario L2A 5X3

Want to try 2 free books from another series! Call 1-800-873-8635 or visit www.ReaderService.com.

*Terms and prices subject to change without notice. Prices do not include sales taxes, which will be charged (if applicable) based on your state or country of residence. Canadian residents will be charged applicable taxes. Offer not valid in Quebec. This offer is limited to one order per household. Books received may not be as shown. Not valid for current subscribers to Love Inspired Romance books. All orders subject to approval. Credit or debit balances in a customer's account(s) may be offset by any other outstanding balance owed by or to the customer. Please allow 4 to 6 weeks for delivery. Offer available while quantities last.

Your Privacy—Your information is being collected by Harlequin Enterprises ULC, operating as Harlequin Reader Service. For a complete summary of the information we collect, how we use this information and to whom it is disclosed, please visit our privacy notice located at corporate.harlequin.com/privacy-notice. From time to time we may also exchange your personal information with reputable third parties. If you wish to opt out of this sharing of your personal information, please visit readerservice.com/consumerschoice or call 1-800-873-8635. **Notice to California Residents**—Under California law, you have specific rights to control and access your data. For more information on these rights and how to exercise them, visit corporate.harlequin.com/california-privacy.

LIR21R

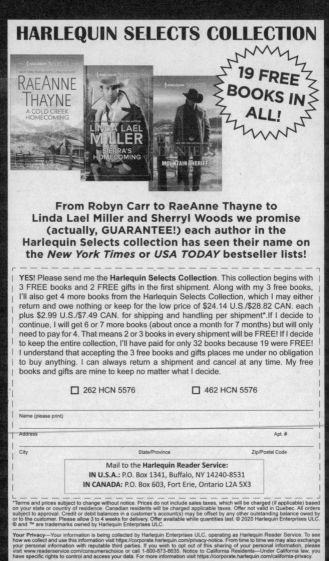